Praise for *Train Shots*

"Evidently, Vanessa Blakeslee was somebody's big se‹
I just don't know how they kept her from us or why t¹
one writes this good the first time out, do they? *Trai*
than a promising first collection by a formidably taler
a haunting story collection of the first order."

~ John Dufresne, author of *No Regrets, Coyote*

"*Train Shots* announces an outstanding new voice. Vanessa
Blakeslee's stories traverse a trilling range of landscapes and voices,
but no matter where her characters find themselves, their struggles
with lost love and loneliness are authentic and engrossing and will
not soon be forgotten."

~ Laura van den Berg, author of *The Isle of Youth*

"In each of the eleven stories in *Train Shots*, Vanessa Blakeslee
immerses her readers in nuanced and impressively imagined
worlds in which characters must choose between loyalty or justice,
between sticking with it or giving up. This is a book populated
with unforgettable, complex characters, each seeking, in one way or
another, a cure for heartbreak."

~ Christine Sneed, author of *Little Known Facts*

"Vanessa Blakeslee's story collection *Train Shots* is the literary
version of a debutante's ball, a lovely introduction to a young writer
just coming into her own."

~ Douglas Glover, author of *Elle* and *Attack of the Copula Spiders*

First Edition. Published by Burrow Press, 2014
Print: burrowpress.com
Web: burrowpressreview.com
Flesh: functionallyliterate.org

Distributed by Itasca Books
5120 Cedar Lake Rd.
Minneapolis, MN 55416
orders@itascabooks.com

The stories in this collection first appeared in the following publications:
"Clock-In" in *Flash Fiction On-line;* "Ask Jesus" in *The Madison Review*
and *Going Down Swinging;* "Welcome, Lost Dogs" in *The Southern
Review;* "Barbecue Rabbit" in *Saranac Review;* "Uninvited Guests" in *The
Wordstock Ten: Finalists from the 2010 Wordstock Short Fiction Competition*;
"The Lung" in *Cimarron Review* and *Split Lip Zine;* "Hospice of the Au
Pair" in *Green Mountains Review;* "Princess of Pop" in *Skidrow Penthouse;*
"The Sponge Diver" in *Toasted Cheese;* "Don't Forget the Beignets" in *The
Louisiana Review;* and "Train Shots" in *Harpur Palate.*

TRAIN SHOTS

stories

VANESSA BLAKESLEE

PAPERBACK bp ORIGINALS

TABLE *of* CONTENTS

Clock In

First we'll clock you in on the computer and then you can shadow me. Your code is the last four digits of your Social, but for tonight you'll need mine to access the tables onscreen. Ever use this system before? It's pretty straightforward. Go ahead—my number is 9791. Open the screen.

So here are all the keys representing the menu. The most important thing to remember, and what's most confusing, is which items come with sour cream and guacamole. For instance, under "Apps"—hit "Apps," then hit "Quesadilla"—you'll see all the different quesadillas you can order: chicken, blackened chicken, black bean. You don't need to modify for sour cream and guacamole because those come with the quesadilla. Also with the fajitas. They're included in the price. But always ask the customer if they would like guacamole or not. It's expensive and we don't like to serve it automatically if we can cut costs.

However, with anything else you *must charge for sour cream and guacamole*. Or if customers want extra. Chimichangas, burritos, combo platters—none of those dinners include either. Make sure you tell customers so they know right off the bat. Now scroll down to "A La Carte." Everything that makes up the combo platters, such as tacos and enchiladas, the customer can order a la carte. And here you'll see the buttons for sour cream and guacamole.

One more thing. Some servers around here, like Erica, have a bad habit of calling in items to the kitchen that they need and not ringing them up. The managers don't like that and you'll get in trouble for calling, "Can I get a sour cream?" when you're supposed to be ringing it in. Erica is on the shit list right now because everyone knows she steals. She's a thief, so watch your drawer. Some servers carry their money on them, but I don't. I doubt Erica steals cash—she's more the type to hook her friends up with free food. But they're on to her, George and Nancy. Actually, you might be Erica's replacement. All I know is, she's walking a thin line with management and they've wanted to fire her for a long time.

The kitchen doesn't like when you call in side items, either. You can be sure George or Nancy will say, "Where's the ticket?" Especially if George is here in the afternoon. See, he's an alcoholic, so around two he can't wait to get off and have his margarita. He'll start snapping at you for practically nothing at all, so don't feel it's your fault. At four, when he clocks out, he goes straight to the bar and downs shots and margaritas. When you're at the service bar he'll lean over and say things that make no sense. Sometimes he sits at the bar all night and gets wasted. But no one else can get as much prep done or deliver orders as quick as when he's clocked-in.

See the skinny little guy behind the line? That's Arthur. He talks and acts like he's Senior Cook, and he'll yak your ear off about how much he picks up everyone else's slack, but he has to take his "break" when we get off the wait list on a Friday night and it's time to clean up. He'll camp out by the Coke machine for thirty minutes and let the dishes pile up if he's on dish. You may have seen him around Winter Park or at the Publix shopping center. He doesn't have a driver's license so he rides a bike. And he lives with about twenty cats. Let me warn you: his house reeks. None of them are spayed or neutered so they multiply like rabbits and he can't take care of them all. My friend Gina adopted one of the kittens last year and it had a big sore oozing on its head and worms crawling out of its butt—this was a cat he gave her! Nice free cat. She spent three hundred dollars at the vet's office. So don't adopt any of Arthur's cats.

Maybe we should go back to learning the system. What happens when you need to take something off a check—say you ring up something by mistake? Then you need to get George or Nancy. George is usually outside doing repairs—he's the only one who gets anything fixed around here. Nancy keeps to the back office because of her smoking. That's something no one talks about, Nancy smoking. She hides back there because she's six months pregnant and doesn't want the regulars to know. But everyone does know, about her smoking.

You're really catching on. I'm so glad, because we're all getting burnt out with the extra shifts. Watch out, though. Erica and I—you'll meet her shortly—we have this joke that soon we'll turn into George or Arthur. We'll sell our cars and move into a duplex in the neighborhood out back. We won't even need bikes to go to work. Hell, George and Arthur can move in with us, Arthur with his twenty cats, and after work at night, and on our vacations, we'll hang around the service bar and make nasty comments to everyone who's in the weeds because we're miserable. So even when we're off we won't leave. We won't have to. The restaurant is all that we need. Sounds funny, I know, but this place will suck you in. Now where were we? That's right. My number is 9791.

Ask Jesus

Halloween night I'm about to run out the front door of my house when I realize the Ask Jesus figurine is missing from my cape pocket. From the driveway Erica yells at me to hurry up, as if I have to be reminded that her managers have been preparing this party for weeks. I ignore her and dash inside—without the figurine and its Magic 8 Ball embedded beneath, my costume won't make sense. I head straight for the bedroom and tear apart the drawers. The front door slams shut and a moment later Erica lurks in the doorway of our room.

"Kind of hard to miss a pink Jesus doll," she says.

"The Ask Jesus is not a doll," I tell her. "He's a limited edition figurine made in 1986. And you could take a look around and help me find him."

"I've got all the parts to my costume." She pets the short black feathers lining the top of her bustier. In a purple-netted skirt, fishnets, and heels, she's supposedly a reincarnation of Gypsy Rose Lee, the burlesque star. I think she looks more like a ballerina on crack.

"Will you check the living room so we can find him and go?" I ask. I flip the bed covers and kneel, dragging my hand underneath.

Instead she sticks her tits in my face and waggles back and forth. "Don't I look great in this?"

"Yeah," I say, "great."

She groans and struts away. "I knew you picked a stupid costume," she says. "Look, why don't you just throw on the Smokey the Bear suit from last year?"

"If I can't find the Ask Jesus, I'm not going to the party," I answer. I tilt the trashcan, but no pink Jesus.

"Fine," she says. Her patent leather heels clop down the hallway and her laughter echoes off the bare walls. My face gets hot, and my eyes go watery with tears, and I think this is no way to spend our first week living together.

•

The next morning I stumble into the living room and find Erica passed out, spiked heels and all, on the beanbag chair. On the coffee table is a ripped open package of vanilla cookies, a glass of Glenfiddich, and a Bettie Page calendar opened to next month, November, with some dates circled. I push away the sticky glass and tug the calendar toward me.

She opens her eyes and lunges for it.

"What time did you get home last night?" I ask, glancing at the dates. The numbers have no apparent significance.

"Did you find him?" she asks.

"What?"

"Oh, God," she says. She sits up and fake feathers from her boa are stuck on her forehead and neck. "The Jesus. Your stupid pink vinyl toy Jesus!"

"You shouldn't call him stupid. It's still Jesus." I chuck the calendar at her feet and say, "I'm going to look for him outside. Maybe I brought him out when I put up the porch display. He could be stuck behind a mummy or something."

She kicks and her heel smacks Bettie Page's head, busts a hole through the paper. I grab her ankles. Her fishnets have runs in both legs. She writhes and almost jabs me in the throat.

"Quit it," I yell. "What the hell's the matter with you?"

"Leave me alone," she whines.

I unbuckle the shoe straps to disarm her. "How was the party?"

"Go ahead and ask Jesus when you find him," she says. "As if you'd care to really know." Shoes off, she kneads her toes against my stomach, then brings her feet to my chest and shoves me away. I grab one foot and start tickling the bottom. "Help me look for him. I'll make you pancakes," I tell her. "Maybe even eggs benedict." She hates cooking, but it's my only other passion besides costumes.

"I don't like your cooking anymore," she says. "And I'm not hungry."

I drop her feet, slide away and leave her in a sulking lump to wander in search of the Ask Jesus.

•

That night I stroll into the bedroom to find Erica reclining with one hand behind her head. The other is massaging her boobs. She's naked, and alternates her massage from one breast to the other every thirty seconds.

"Do you really have to do that?" I ask.

"If I don't, the silicon hardens," she replies. "I don't want them to get like rocks. You heard the doctor."

I step into the closet and turn on the light. "My opinion didn't matter much, if you recall."

"Well, I like them," she says. "You have to admit they made my costume a success."

"I still haven't found the Ask Jesus," I say. "Imagine if he's right here, in front of my face."

"Why don't you just give up?" she calls from the bed. "Buy a new one."

"That's not the point," I say. "He was here, and now he's gone. It's not like he ascended." I rummage in the plastic storage bins piled high with Mardi Gras beads, a lunch box, a baton, the Smokey the Bear hat.

"I don't even understand what your costume was supposed to be," she says. The sheets rustle and I glance up at her moving towards me, her fake breasts planted like waxen udders. "Who's the Bible Blazer anyway?"

"He's the super hero of the Bible Belt," I explain. "The Ask Jesus is central to the costume and stands for the entire 'What would Jesus do?' movement. Without it, the costume fails in purpose."

"You ought to have an Ask Mary doll in your other pocket," she says. "To fairly represent women."

"Ask Mary wouldn't be the same as Ask Jesus," I say, shaking my head. "Not at all. Are you just going to stand there naked or help me find him?"

"And what's this?" She picks up the belt I made for the Bible Blazer costume and holds it far away, as if it's a poisonous snake. I had fixed a miniature Gideons Bible—the free ones handed out in malls—over the buckle.

"Get out of my way if you're not going to help," I tell her.

"You could help me," she says. Still holding the belt, she reaches down with her other hand and pinches her nipple. "Aren't breasts a lot more exciting?"

We stare at one another in the doorway of the closet. I peel the belt away from her hand. "What happened at that party? You still haven't told me."

"Nothing," she says. "It wasn't important after all." She

looks down at her breasts. Then she does something strange. She slaps them, first lightly but then harder. I watch, amazed. Her lip pouts in anger. She keeps slapping as if I'm not even there. I step forward and grab her by the shoulders, but she brushes past me into the master bathroom. Seconds later the shower is running. I sit on the edge of the bed, unsure of what just happened.

From the shower Erica gives a cry and a *thump* sounds against the bathroom door. I leap up and push the door open a few more inches.

The Ask Jesus rolls into view.

•

That night Erica takes a sleeping pill and snores soundly within minutes, leaving me to lie awake and wonder: did she hide the Ask Jesus on purpose? I sit up and turn on the lamp. Even the dim light hurts my eyes. While I wait for them to adjust, I take the Ask Jesus off the bedside table and study him. He's about the same height and weight of Mrs. Butterworth and an appropriate Easter pink. He wears a pansy-ass Jesus expression paired with long hippy hair that I don't really find acceptable, but it's Jesus, just the same. So what am I waiting for? I close my eyes and form my question. *Am I right about what's happened to my wife?* Then I flip him upside down and stare into the window beneath his pink robes and sandaled feet for the response to appear. The water sloshes and I have to hold him underneath the lamp in order to read the bobbing message: It is decidedly so.

•

Barely a week later, I find the Bettie Page calendar in the garage trash, big red Xs over Bettie's face, tits, and ass, although the page with the marked dates is missing. Erica starts wearing loose button-downs with the sleeves rolled up and making big breakfasts in the morning, even during the week—waffles, coffee, eggs-any-which-way.

Erica gets up on Sunday and says she's going to check out a non-denominational church down the road. I stay home and complete an online dating profile with the requirement, "Ladies with enhancements of any make or model need not apply." As I complete the series of personal questions, I consult the Ask Jesus perched atop my dresser, found but not forgotten. His answers seem to match my own. This gives me a good feeling.

I have just finished when Erica returns. She idly picks up the Ask Jesus and strokes his face. "Glad I found him," she says.

"Did you?" I ask.

"Of course," she replies. "Under the bathroom sink. The cleaning lady must have thought he was some type of soap dispenser."

I doubt this is true. I suspect Erica didn't want me to go to the party because her lover would be there, so she hid Jesus on me. Then they had a falling out, which she's now trying to cover up.

I wave for her to hand over Jesus so that I may ask him myself. *Is there any hope to save my marriage?* I plead silently.

His response: Pray harder.

"You act as if God is really communicating with you through that doll," Erica says with a snort. "It's absurd."

"Oh, yeah? Maybe you should ask him if my ways are so absurd." I set Ask Jesus on the table and scoot him forward to face her.

For a moment she remains still, as if squared off in a showdown with the figurine, but then she grabs it. She twists and shakes his body a few times and turns him on end. "Is my husband as foolish as I think he is, Jesus?" she asks in a steady but mocking tone.

"Allow me to predict his answer," I say. "*Don't count on it.* Unless you want to confess. Tell me what's been going on with you these last few months."

She stares for a long time at the message but doesn't show it to me. "No, I don't," she says. "What I want is a clean slate. And enough with this Jesus doll."

"No questions asked," I say slowly, deliberating. "That's asking a lot. Especially when I have no idea whether or not you still love me."

She nods. "What about you?" she asks, her voice small. She looks strikingly penitent. Maybe it's the shirt, *sans* cleavage. Her eyes without makeup, searching mine.

I rise and pause just long enough to rest my hand on her head. "What do you think?" I ask. Then I walk out to the porch, banging the screen door, and toss Ask Jesus in the trash can with the other Halloween decorations, soaked and wilted after days of rain.

Welcome, Lost Dogs

Behind the stable, the afternoon sun cast its shadow across the mountainsides. On the rocky road winding to the ridge above my ranch, a noisy backhoe scooped the dirt away; another gringo's purchase of paradise was going up to loom over the clusters of tin-roofed Tico houses crowded below. Fifteen years ago, we were the only ones here. But even then, my husband and I would shake our heads. More and more people born, and the ones already living didn't have enough to eat. Same with the animals. So I decided against having children. And then his son was still running around, chin quivering over scrapes from soccer cleats. That was enough.

The stableboy shook his head at me. He explained that he slept in the back of the building, far from the road, and only heard the wind and the horses. Was he lying? He was fairly new, and young, about fourteen. He had been there only two months, hired after the last stableboy, also Nicaraguan, drifted elsewhere.

"I want you to ride up and down the road," I said. "Ask everyone you pass if they saw this happen. Tell them there's a reward."

His eyes flickered, and he shifted his stance. "How much?" he asked.

"I don't know," I said. "But there will be one. More for the yellow Lab, *el perro d'oro*. You know the one?"

He nodded, scuffed the heel of his boot in the sawdust. "The one that brings things back when you throw them," he said.

•

At the *soda* just outside our gate, the street dogs lolled in the shade. They nipped at fleas and sniffed underneath each other's tails. I told my story to the *soda* owner. He just shrugged. He saw nothing, doesn't open until seven. But he asked how much of a reward for the stolen dogs. Was I just a crazy gringa to this man, standing behind his counter of cigarettes and lotto tickets? He knew me; I'd bought ice from him for years. But had he ever before seen anyone like me, trembling and shiny eyed over a bunch of dogs?

"How much can you win at the lotto?" I asked.

"Ten thousand dollars, U.S." he said.

"I'll offer a hundred thousand colones for the dogs," I told him. For a maid or a stableboy or a *soda* clerk, that amounted to two hundred dollars, or almost a month's wages.

Outside, the thick scent of cooking drifted out the windows of the houses. But I wasn't hungry. There would be no feeding the dogs that night, no checking for ticks. This settled over me, as strange as putting on long sleeves after days of too much sun at the beach. Up until a year ago, I ran a small animal shelter in Piedades. We fixed animals for cheap. But keeping all the animals in cages bothered me, and there were so many dogs brought in we had to turn away dozens every day, so that by night, when I climbed into my car, I fought back tears. Finally I sold the business to a vet who needed the space. I built the dog pen on my property so that at least the ones I rescued could have room to run, to live.

What would happen if I didn't find the dogs? Would I sell the house to a green gringo with palm trees in his eyes, and leave like so many old friends? Because wherever you go, there you are, as my husband used to say. The dogs had been my passion. But even if the dogs were found, I didn't know if my heart had room for more, after this.

I ducked into doorways and questioned pregnant mothers with toddlers slung onto one hip. Both the mothers and babies displayed the round, clear faces of youth. I zigzagged through the young men with book bags hoisted onto their backs at the bus stop, until the last Tico kid boarded the bus and shot me a wincing smile. I waved over the farmer clopping down the street on his Paso Fino. He stopped to talk. But even though he had awakened before dawn, he knew nothing. "Bandidos are like ghosts," he said. "And the winds were loud in the middle of the night."

So I trudged back toward home. Mongrel dogs scurried at the ends of driveways, barking at me but mostly at one another, warning, *This is mine, that's yours. Feed me soon or I'm going to lie down and die.* I imagined my corral of rescued dogs running helter-skelter and snapping at each other's heels. When I first found *el perro d'oro* three months ago, he was stretched out in the ditch not far from here, with a cardboard box collapsed on top of him. Whoever dropped him there had left a bag of food torn open next to him. The bone of his hind leg split through the bloodied skin; I had to turn my eyes away. Later the vet said it had been broken in six places. The maids called him Orito, little golden one.

I continued through the gauntlet of canines, torn by my desires. A part of me wanted to scoop up each dog and carry him to my pen, one by one, until the space returned to life. But the other part of me, weighed down, wanted to charge up to each dog and yell, *Go home! Go home!*

So I did. I rushed one, then another, bent down and chucked stones from the end of my driveway at the mutts trailing my footsteps. I yelled until the dogs scattered, slinking down side roads or squeezing through fences. I yelled even though they had nowhere to go and did not know the word *home*.

I hit the button on my key chain to close the gate, and from between the wrought-iron bars I glimpsed a male mutt with a matted orange coat pissing a golden arch onto my driveway. Above him hung the faded sign: BIENVENIDOS, PERROS PERDIDOS.

•

With the maids' help, I called neighbors and the handful of shelters that existed in San José. We placed ads in the classifieds of the *Tico Times*, the English-language newspaper, and *La Nación* with the reward. We made posters and fixed them at the bus stops and in the windows of the churches and the *soda* on the corner. We didn't bother to call the police because they could do nothing for such a crime. The human problem was too much for them.

But days passed, then a week, and we heard nothing.

My cook lit the candles in her little kitchen shrine and prayed for the dogs. I prayed and cried, too, only I kept my tears to the bedroom or the shower. My prayers were filled with questions—Why, this senseless thing? Why all of them, if someone just wanted *el perro d'oro* to breed? To feed the rest to a ring of fighting dogs back in the thieves' home country?

I tossed at night, unable to sleep because of the dogs and the ceaseless rattling winds that sounded like my heart. Just before dawn, the winds would die down and I would sleep at last, until one of the maids knocked at my door. On a particular morning, this happened much earlier than usual; the roosters had just begun to crow in the pitch black. "El teléfono," the maid said. "Los perros perdidos."

Another prank, I thought. I fell back against the down pillows with the phone an inch away from my ear. "Dígame," I said.

The caller sounded like a young girl, perhaps a teenager. She said her brother and his friends had stolen the dogs, and she had overheard them talking about how they had taken them from a rich gringa's house in the hills of Salitral. The brother and his friends had left the night before for Panama. She didn't know when the men would be back, but she didn't think they would keep the dogs there too much longer. Her brother would likely beat her and throw her out of the house, but she didn't care. She needed the reward money to buy her baby's formula. In the background, I overheard yelps and the rattle of cages. I even thought that I recognized the bark of *el perro d'oro.*

She gave me directions to a place in Alajuelita, and I asked her for the streets two more times just to be sure. I told her I wouldn't go there until the middle of the day, it wasn't safe, but she pushed me to come right away.

With shaking fingers, I dressed in jeans and a baggy sweat shirt. I pulled my hair back into a ponytail, the whole time asking myself, What am I doing, for these dogs? Alajuelita, near downtown, was the poorest and most dangerous barrio of San José. One time my ex-husband and I had taken a wrong turn coming down the hill from Escazú, and the long, winding road spit us out right in the heart of Alajuelita. Even though night had just fallen, gangs of young men roamed the trash-filled sidewalks, and the shantytown went on for miles. We kept driving into the labyrinth of unmarked streets, just like those of all the other towns and barrios of Costa Rica—only driving into Alajuelita with a new Peugeot was like sticking a rabbit into my dogs' pen. I recalled my ex-husband smoking one cigarette after another down to the filter as he drove on, trying to find us a way out, only to stop at yet another intersection which looked identical to the last. At one stop sign, crackheads descended on our car and rapped on the windows. Finally I spotted a city bus, and we followed it to a main road, out of that hell.

I decided to bring one of my maids with me, a Nica who couldn't drive but knew the poor neighborhoods near downtown. I didn't bring a purse, just tucked the reward money in ten-thousand colon notes in a baggie which I hid in the waist of my jeans. I tossed leashes into the back of the old Galloper we used on the ranch, and the holster with my ex-husband's old .45 onto the front seat. During the whole winding journey along Calle Vieja toward Alajuelita, I grappled with the feeling that I didn't quite know what I was doing. I replayed the girl's voice again and again, trying to remember if any part of the conversation sounded untrue, another hoax pulled on gringos. But whenever I replayed the call, the barking in the background drowned out any hint of a possible lie amongst all of her rattled-off specifics. Caring for the dogs had become a practice which sustained me, much more than I ever realized. And in the recent days without the dogs, I felt as if splinters were driving up through my skin.

•

I thought the sun would come up faster, but it didn't. We entered Alajuelita in the dim light, the dawn just turning the sky between the mountains a pale gray. At a stop sign, we paused to go over directions; thirty seconds into the neighborhood and already the streets of the slum had us lost. A lone crackhead, barefoot and wearing only a long, ragged T-shirt, approached the Galloper. The woman's face twitched and her eyes rolled around; she cradled a bowl of wet rice against her chest and shoveled handfuls of the glop into her mouth. She banged against my window with the flat of her hand.

I pressed the gas, sent the skeletal woman reeling, and didn't look back.

Then we spotted the *soda* the caller had described in her directions—the gate pulled down and locked, the building painted with graffiti. I parked on the street, pulled up the hood of my sweat shirt, and told the maid to wait. Then I strapped the holster underneath my clothes and secured the gun in place; before this, I had only carried a side arm while riding cross-country up in Nicaragua. The maid climbed out, insisting that I not go alone, but I yelled at her to get back in the truck. Then I locked the doors and headed to the alleyway which led to the back of the *soda*. This was where the girl said she would meet me with the dogs. And I heard the restless sounds of animals, the clinking of chains and claws on concrete nearby, behind the high wire fences.

A few junkies were sleeping and picking through garbage in the alleyway. I hurried past them with my chin low and my hands tucked underneath my armpits. In the back of the *soda* stood a group of lean-to shanties. The yard was paved with plastic bottles and metal scraps; the air reeked of piss and trash. A woman cooked over an open fire underneath her tin roof. But I kept heading deeper into the thicket of shanties, closer to the sounds of the caged animals.

A young woman stepped out from one of the shanties. "Buscando los perros?" she asked. She yawned; her crooked mouth was full of gaping black holes. Then she looked me over with slit eyes. "El dinero, ahora mismo," she demanded.

"Dónde están los perros?" I asked. "I left the money in the car."

She blocked my path and waved two dirty fingers to someone in the darkness. A squirrel of a man emerged, his exposed chest and limbs as sinewy as barbed wire. He lifted up a rope with a noose at the end, and the noose choked the neck of a mutt—a gasping, skinny street dog no bigger than a baby goat. "Give us *el dinero*," he said. "Or we do this to your dogs, right in front of you."

My heart lurched in my chest with fear and horror. But the mongrel wasn't mine. The golden yellow of the dawning sun gleamed off the roofs of the shanties. I had known better than to come here. "You don't have the dogs, *cabroncito*," I said. "I'm going."

"*El dinero, señora*, or we'll do this to you," the man said. He whipped out a switchblade. Then he lowered the half-dead dog, the fur already gathering flies, and slit its throat. The creature yelped, then fell silent. Blood poured down the coat, dripped from the ribs to the trash-carpeted mud.

I stepped back. The man tossed the rope and the dog to the ground, inched forward and held up the knife. He extended his other hand, rubbing his thumb and forefinger together. "Dáme el dinero ahora," he said.

My heart thundered in my ears as I took in the scars from street fighting that ran up and down the man's bare torso and forearms. I reached underneath my sweatshirt, pulled out the gun, and fired two shots into the dirt and trash a meter away from the man's feet. A chicken with one wing ran along the ground between us, and I spun around and fled. The smell of burning trash turned my stomach, and I slipped on slimy papers and rot as I dashed through the alleyway. A chorus of dogs barked throughout the barrio—this was the sound I had heard as I journeyed into the slum. Only when I jumped into the Galloper did I look out and find that no one had been chasing me, and I fought to catch my breath as I peeled out. When I looked over at the maid, she had taken the gun from my lap. She raised it to her chest and gripped the handle with both hands, her dark eyes wide.

I cursed myself the whole way back to Salitral for falling into such a trap. The other side of the highway bottlenecked with commuter traffic on the way into downtown. I avoided looking into the doorways of the shacks as I sped past them and up the hill to my ranch. In that moment, I wished that the hovels would burn to rubble and ash and all the poor within them.

•

My ex-husband's voice rippled up and down, as if from an old tape gone wonky from overuse. His body was so riddled from the Parkinson's that he could no longer wipe his own ass. "Why are you still down there?" he asked. He said I should go to France. The French treated dogs well. Dogs were allowed on the high-speed trains and in the malls in France.

"Moving doesn't solve everything," I said.

"Yeah, well, would've been no life for you here, with me like this," he said. He lived in a retirement community in south Florida, having recently traded round-the-clock maids for nurses. He said, "I still have friends in France if you want to go back to Marseilles."

"That was another life," I told him.

"Well, so what?" he asked. "You can choose again."

"I don't want to go back to anywhere, okay?" I said. But just before I hung up, I paused and said, "I love you."

•

One night I dreamed of the dogs. The bandidos had shut them up in a tight, black space, and the barks were mixed with desperate growls. They pressed their faces up to a window and licked, shrill whines escaping their throats. I stood on the other side but I couldn't break the glass; I couldn't help them. It was so dark that I couldn't see any of their eyes. Where was *el perro d'oro*? But at last I shuddered awake, and the same dark feeling—of hunger, feces, stifling air—clutched my chest.

I flung off the covers and dragged my suitcase from the closet. In the stillness before dawn, the first rooster crowed, his cry carried by the gusts of wind. I packed cargo pants, toiletries but no makeup, riding boots. The leg of *el perro d'oro* would have been healed by now. He was supposed to be a present for my stepson.

All that week since the hoax in Alajuelita, I'd jumped at every phone call, and I was tired of people trying to pass off abandoned litters of puppies for my stolen mutts. I avoided the lower end of the property because I couldn't bear to see the desolate sandlot. Now, I just wanted to forget the dogs. So I decided to go up to Nicaragua for a week, to my stepson's *finca* outside Managua where he raised horses.

The last time I had spoken to him was two months ago, before Christmas. He had called to tell me a tenant farmer had beaten one of his favorite dogs to death and to ask my advice on whether to throw the family off the land. Most of his farmers had barely survived the winter because all they had planted the year before was yuca and frijoles, and he wasn't sure that such ignorance should meet further harsh punishment. I said, "Karma's got to be harsh. How else are we supposed to evolve?" He sighed, sounding much older than a kid twenty-four years old, and said he just wasn't sure.

•

"You don't have to live in a third-world country," I told him. "Come down to Costa Rica and visit."

"Costa Rica is too crowded," he said. "Too many gringos. There's still a sense of adventure here. The Wild West."

He always said this, even though he was a blue-eyed American who had spent all his school vacations in California and Virginia. But he was more Latino male than gringo, kept one girlfriend in this town and another in that one. Or maybe that was due to his father's French blood. But he bought nine hundred acres in Nicaragua when he turned twenty-one, used all of his inheritance. He claimed to be self-sufficient, that he wanted to grow his own crops for when the rest of the earth's topsoil turned to dust and lawlessness broke out in the cities. I wondered if he really believed this or if he was just another person caught between countries, like me. Except every day at dawn he poured that spaciousness in which he drifted over himself like a pitcher of water, while I pushed the pitcher away.

•

Several days later in Nicaragua, I was riding across the slopes of my stepson's *finca* next to one of his jefes. Our horses kicked up dust so I pulled my kerchief up to just underneath my eyes. Jocote trees bordered the road on both sides. From the crests of the hills we could see for miles. On the hillside opposite ours, a couple, brown and weathered as coconuts, tossed seeds onto parched furrows. The woman's threadbare dress hugged her knees; both she and her husband treaded the stony dirt barefoot. The old man's rippled chest bared his ribs as he bent over. They planted in silence. We trotted by and the woman gave us a sidelong glance, but nothing more. What did she see in just that glimpse—horses with rounded bellies and muscled legs, worn but well-made boots, me with my pistol at my side in case we ran into trouble?

And run into trouble we did, at the bottom of the hill. Two men and two *chicos*, probably their sons and not yet teenagers, were felling trees and chopping wood. The smaller boy bundled wood with long pieces of cord, his fingers flying. We steered the horses through the jocote trees, right into the middle of their operation. They froze and lowered their axes. Sweat glistened on their jaws and forearms.

The jefe spoke to them first, asking if they knew whose land this was, but they stared at me. Even with my dark hair and bronzed skin, I was still a gringa, riding the countryside with no husband and a weapon at my side.

The jefe stopped talking and nodded in my direction. I held my horse steady and sat up tall, and the big Spanish beauty tossed his head, the high midday sun casting his huge shadow over the thieves. It was my turn to address them.

"Who gave you permission to cut this wood?" I asked.

"No one," one of the men said. He cast his gaze to the ground. "We need firewood," he said. "My brother didn't think anyone would mind."

"So this is what you show your sons, how to steal?" I asked. "Because that's my wood."

But the men and the *chicos* still didn't look at me. They tucked their chins to their chests and said nothing.

I asked the jefe, "What should we do?" Looking at the thieves, I said, "Should we shoot them for stealing?"

The boys' heads shot up, but the men just stared at the dirt and didn't move. Finally one of them touched his forehead and grabbed the shoulder of the nearest boy.

"How would you like it if I rode onto your land and took

something of yours?" I asked. "Maybe I take your corn. Or maybe your chickens. Maybe I even steal your dogs." I rested my hand on the gun.

The man dropped his hand from the shoulder of the boy and spoke; his mouth was full of holes and his teeth the color of a muddy river. "We will leave all the wood and go home," he said.

I thought of the bare-chested man in the alleyway, how he held up the dead dog at the end of his rope with one hand, a knife in the other, pointed at me, and all the anger and fear I had felt rushed back. Once again the same gun rested in my holster. And I pictured how easy it would be right here in this clearing in the middle of lawless, forgotten Nicaragua to point the gun at any one of these thieves, shoot to kill, and rid the world of their ignorance.

But I asked him, "What will I do with all this cut wood? And how do I know you won't come back and steal from me tomorrow?" The eyes of the boys widened, and they looked up at the men and waited.

"We won't come back," the taller of the boys said. "We only needed a little wood."

Everyone fell silent. Some farmer nearby was burning garbage; the smoke invaded my nostrils. The jefe looked at me. I told them that we had plenty of wood we needed cleared away, but these trees here were good and must be left alone. I asked the men and boys if they understood and they nodded in unison. I told them to come to the big house, and the jefes would show them where they might cut all the wood they could carry. I asked again if they understood and their heads bobbed up and down. Then I said, "If you needed wood, why didn't you just ask?"

The four of them just stared at me, like strays that show up on the doorstep.

The jefe and I steered our horses back to the road, picking through the cut branches and logs. I glanced over my shoulder before we rounded the bend. The men and boys scrambled to heave bunches of wood over their shoulders. Then they scurried into the jungle and out of sight.

•

We passed the spot again on our return ride home, the clearing deserted but for a pack of wild dogs that lingered underneath the jocote trees bordering the road. Some sniffed one another, nipping and playing, but others fought. They tackled each other; the victims yelped. One dog trotted off to the side and choked down the little green jocote fruit, and I laughed.

The jefe laughed at me, laughing.

"I didn't know dogs ate jocotes," I said.

He replied, "Starving dogs will eat anything." And we kept riding.

•

We passed the farm, too, where the old couple had crouched in the dirt. But now the field sat empty and covered in long shadows as the sun stained the western sky a pink grapefruit color. The world is a field of stones for most human beings, and the more they dig up the earth, the more stones they find and their stomachs rumble with hunger. That night the thieving farmers and their sons would build a fire and cook their first hot meal in days. For how many nights had they spoken to each other in darkness, unable to see one another's faces, the schoolbooks littering the floor, the two boys huddled under blankets as the blackness enveloped them, hour after hour?

My dogs lay in the darkness somewhere, in a heap on top of one another, too exhausted and too broken of spirit to keep barking for help. If they were suffering, I hoped they would be killed soon—if they weren't, I wanted them to keep barking so someone might hear them. I had stopped for the broken-legged Lab, hadn't I?

A figure appeared up ahead on the side of the road, but I couldn't see his or her head because of the great bundle of branches on the person's back. The bundle was so big that from a distance it almost looked comical: a tree-creature made of branches with two brown legs trotting underneath, thin as an insect's. But when our horses caught up, I recognized the woman who was planting earlier. Through the leafy branches that bent over her head and partially hid her face, I saw her eyes. She had gathered up the remaining branches that the thieves left behind. And this time as I passed, she stared at me. She wouldn't let me go; her eyes didn't even blink.

We climbed the hill and lumbered down the other side, and I still felt that stare boring between my shoulder blades.

•

Back at my stepson's place, over tamales and beer, I spilled the problem of the men stealing wood. But my stepson just shook his head and brushed his hands on the tops of his jeans. He had stumbled across this before. A couple of months ago, he told his workers to spread the word that whoever wanted wood could cut down trees from a certain area where the underbrush needed clearing out, and he would charge them a price they could afford—very cheap. He even came up with a bonus: for every four cords of wood cut and paid for, the fifth cord was free. He showed the schoolchildren of his illiterate *finca* bosses how to write the customers' names in a special notebook, mark Xs in columns to keep track of the cords of wood.

"So has it worked out?" I asked.

"Nope," my stepson replied. "They just steal." He smirked over the rim of his beer and exchanged a look with the jefe, who shrugged.

"I'd shoot the men who stole my dogs," I said. "But I'll never find out who they were or see my dogs again."

"That's right, you won't," he said. He sipped his beer. "Dad's dying," he said.

"I know," I said.

"I'm going to see him in a few weeks," he said. "Why don't you come to the States for a while?"

But I didn't answer. I hadn't forgotten the phone call to my ex-husband, just like I hadn't forgotten the dogs; some things just slip to the back of the mind easier than others. And I still couldn't forget the dogs. I would go home, but where was home? Was it here with my stepson, or back in Costa Rica? Was it in Florida, at my ex-husband's side? Home was all and none of those places. I pushed away from the table and stepped out onto the *rancho*. I scanned the stars until my neck hurt, not only for my lost dogs, but for this lost world.

•

The next day, my stepson rode next to me. I wanted to show him the place where the thieves had been felling trees. We passed the field belonging to the old man and woman, but they were nowhere in sight; the tin shack stood still, the sun glaring off its battered roof and sides. I shaded my eyes and scanned their patch of land for a glimpse of the old man's bony chest or the woman's gray head cropping up between the patched sheets strung along the clothesline. I asked my stepson where they might be.

He shrugged and stared ahead at the road. "Hauling water," he said. He removed his oversized black sunglasses, movie-star style, and rode with his cowboy hat hanging from its strings down his back. He squinted, and the skin around his eyes crinkled like rivulets. Since our last visit, the sun had mapped his face even more deeply, the creases those of a man who had already spent years taming brush and lassoing horses. "That's the old man who killed the dog in December," he said.

The horses' hooves thudded against the earth and the trees droned with the buzz of thousands of insects. Thirsty, I fumbled for the water bottle tucked at my waist, opposite my gun, and drank. "You didn't kick them off?" I finally asked. "You don't think an old man who runs around killing dogs might be trouble?"

"They ate the dog," he said. "When I showed up here to confront him, the woman was boiling the bones in a pot. She was too ashamed and upset to look at me. Those two were sacks of skin."

I gripped the reins tighter and the stallion's ears shot up, awaiting a command, but we just rode on, my heart thudding as hard as when I ran into the center of the vacant pen, screaming for my poor dogs. I asked, "What did you do?"

He replied, "I bought bags of seeds and gathered all the farmers together and told them to plant more so they wouldn't starve. Some are open to planting new crops, but some are too afraid to take the risk."

"You're kidding," I said with a laugh. But he didn't laugh or even look my way.

We were farther down the road now, and the spot came into view: more stumps, fallen branches, missing trees. But I wasn't angry anymore, just sad.

"Lots of Indian blood in the Nicas," my stepson said. He drummed the side of his head with his knuckles and raised his eyebrows at me knowingly. He jumped off his horse and reached down for a long branch blocking the way. "Wood belongs to everyone nearby who needs it, they tell me," he said. "But why won't they take the damn brush that needs to be cleared out? Because they're idiots, that's why." And with both hands, he heaved the branch to the side with such force that the ripe jocotes flung off.

I pulled up on my horse and watched him toss more branches in the brush, the breeze carrying the smoke of the cooking fires that burned in the neighboring hillsides. I pictured the men and the two boys who stood looking up at me in this very spot yesterday, and then my Nicaraguan stableboy at home unbolting the main gate and waving in the dog thieves for a few extra colones to send to his family. I saw the faceless thieves wrestling with the darting dogs, hurling them into the back of the van or truck, young men my stepson's age. But those men were the kind who had spent their whole lives in the slums of Alajuelita, in San José, or crossed the border from Nicaragua or Colombia or other places like this. Then I pictured a dark warehouse, the colones exchanged for the caged dogs so that the young thieves could go down to the market and buy their beans and rice.

"Maybe I should move here," I called over to my stepson. "I could help you with the farmers."

He laughed. "Do you really want to do that?" he said. "Sorry. But you can't stand Costa Rica half of the time."

"That's the first time I've heard you laugh in a year," I said. "Glad I'm so funny to you."

"Oh, quit it," he said. "Stay another week, then tell me how much there is to laugh about in this place." He straightened up and cracked a branch over his knee.

·

That night, underneath the cornucopia of stars, my stepson joined me outside the *rancho*. In his part of Nicaragua, the farms had no electricity. None would likely exist until he paid to run the lines to his land, but I doubted he ever would. He preferred to live like this, rough and raw underneath the stars. I might have brought all the dogs here, and they would have been romping and running after lizards instead of lost. "I'm not going to rescue dogs anymore," I said suddenly. A lantern blazed between us, the rest of the night pitch black but for the light of the stars from above.

"When's the last time you saw Dad?" my stepson asked. His voice sounded like stones had caught in his throat.

"A year ago, when he left. The last time you did."

From the darkness below the *rancho*, the horses stomped and whinnied in the stable. The dogs barked a cacophony after them; somewhere off in the distance, guns fired. My stepson said, "I hope you don't beat yourself up about that. You're twenty years younger than him. You can still ride, for God's sake. He always wanted you to have a great life."

"I know," I said. "But all this time I've spent saving dogs. Maybe I should have been helping people."

And I looked out into the blackness, and the events that had marked the inevitable decline of our life shone back, each one as singular as a star but clustered together in my memory. One day we saddled up for a ride only to find my ex-husband could no longer mount his horse; another day, he could not climb the slight slope just outside our kitchen to check on his herb garden, even with the help of a cane. The last night we ate out at our favorite Italian restaurant in Escazú, I jumped up every two minutes to wipe the salad falling out of his wobbling mouth, and I looked at him across the table and told him, no more. It was the end of everything we had shared, and after several lives scattered across different continents, no small thing. But I was forty-eight years old and not ready to turn over my days to his round-the-clock care. At first he tried to persuade me to go with him to Miami. But I couldn't picture myself there, driving amidst all those high-rises and convertibles to watch nurses in pressed white cotton ease the man I loved up and out of his bed to the chair, to watch the journey he must now make to take a simple walk outside. By the time we found the retirement home, he insisted that we get divorced. After all, he said, he might linger on for years.

I remembered our good-bye: my soon-to-be ex-husband kissing the delicate leaves of his cilantro, breathing in the last of their aroma, embracing the maids one by one, then our son, before pressing his trembling lips hard against mine.

•

For nearly the entire trip back to Costa Rica, I thought of *el perro d'oro*. I had doted on him throughout his recovery: checking his shattered leg for infection and changing the dressing twice a day, frying up chicken livers to mix with old rice for his meals, carrying him outside to relieve himself until he gained strength. As he grew stronger, I tossed him tennis balls and he hobbled after them, his stiff-wrapped leg sticking out as he ran on his three good ones. Of all my street dogs, he was the only one that I brought into the house, ever. This was almost a year after my husband's departure from the country he had once insisted would be our ideal home. "The Ticos call it *la pura vida*," he had said to me, years before, over a bottle of wine in Marseilles.

And I had only put *el perro d'oro* out in the pen for the first time the evening before the bandidos stole the dogs. His leg had mostly healed; I had wanted to get him acquainted with other mutts before bringing him to my stepson's farm, with his mix of purebreds and mongrels. At the time the bandidos stole the dogs, I had arranged homes for half of them.

From Nicaragua, I drove the rest of the long and winding route through the mountains of northeastern Costa Rica, past the volcanoes and the coffee farms. Trucks passed ahead of me on the blind curves. Perhaps when we don't need a person or a creature or even a place anymore, it leaves us and doesn't return. Perhaps that thing is even bound to leave because we love it so intensely, and nothing can be intense for long. And from there a gap opens up so that we may see something else in need of our attention. So we don't get a good-bye or an explanation. What's gone is gone; that gate remains shut. There are three kinds of grief: the grief of the definite, for what once was and is now gone; the grief of the indefinite, where there are no answers and so the worst is suspected; and the grief of the inevitable, for what must be lost and whose future must be abandoned.

By the time I descended from the misty hillsides lined with coffee shrubs and into the traffic of Alajuela, the yelps of my dogs faded into the distant corners of my memory, like the sound of laundry flapping somewhere in the wind. And when I drove up the road to Salitral, I didn't avert my eyes from the people descending the hill on foot when their gazes met mine.

•

Back home, my stableboy and a couple more Nicaraguan *chicos* I hired for the job raked the dank earth of the dog pen into a pile. I set fire to the dung and bones, the reward posters shrinking and curling black on top. The Nicaraguans spit out jocote seeds as they worked. They shouted to one another, and in one fell swoop, pulled down the chain link fence.

Barbecue Rabbit

Layla and her son Ethan, fifteen, had been unpacking boxes at their new house in Northampton County when she brought up the possibility of Ethan visiting his father in prison. She'd been afraid that her proposal would set Ethan off on one of his episodes, and sure enough, he hit her in the face. Then he grabbed one of the box cutters and tore into the couches. Stuffing erupted and she fled, barricading herself in her new bedroom upstairs while awaiting the police. Ethan spent the next two weeks at the Lehigh Valley branch of KidsPeace, a nonprofit organization for troubled youth. If she didn't find a way to stop her son's behavior, she feared he'd kill someone.

But after Ethan's return home two uneventful weeks passed. Layla allowed him to go with his older cousins on her ex-husband's side to the annual Fourth of July picnic. She showed up later and was surprised to see the teenage boys laughing and passing around a rabbit. Ethan had named the rabbit Barbecue and set it scampering around the campsite for the younger cousins to play with. She hadn't seen Ethan smile in weeks; maybe all he needed was to spend more time with relatives his age, like Will, who would leave for Penn State in August. There was still time. She fetched a beer, her first since the move.

All afternoon the rabbit, a hefty New Zealand white, tried to escape the delighted shouts of the seven-year-old twin cousins as they chased it along the shore of the large pond. The creature appeared to hate the close proximity of the water, retreating to the grass whenever it got the chance, but the kids jumped and dived like rodeo clowns and confined it to the sand.

Later, Layla would recall that none of the grown-ups had paid much attention to the swimming beach. They had set up camp around a pavilion one hundred yards away, under the same alcove of trees chosen every year as the center of the Fourth of July picnic. The aunts reclined in lawn chairs; the cracking open of Yuengling cans peppered the drone of their long-awaited gossip. The uncles played softball in a nearby field until sundown, when the hot dog roast would start.

A gentle hand clutched her arm and she jolted. "It's Ethan," Will said. "He says he's going to cook the rabbit for dinner." She shot out of her seat; beer gushed over the grass. They hurried to the narrow beach, and even though the sun beat on her neck and arms, she shivered.

On the far shore Ethan hoisted the rabbit overhead. The kids were yelling in protest and ramming into his torso, tiny fists balled. He brandished a Swiss Army knife and positioned the squirming rabbit underneath his arm like a football. Will and Layla broke into a run, both of them yelling for Ethan to stop. But he headed for the pines beyond. Will charged ahead, but Layla paused to catch her breath. She had known better than to bring her son to the picnic this year, after what had happened moving week. And now this.

The twins' parents whom Layla didn't know well, cousins of her ex-husband, backed their Subaru up to the kiddy camp, climbed out, and puttered around. The husband picked up the strewn plastic beach toys, and the mother tried to calm the sobbing girl while the twin boy pounded the sand, howling. The two mothers exchanged glances. "I'm so sorry," Layla said. The twins' mother said nothing.

Will came striding out of the woods—the white rabbit, alive, cradled in his arms.

"Where's Ethan?" Layla asked.

"Back there." Will motioned toward the pines. "He was going to slit its throat, but I told him no way, that rabbit'll scream. If he wants barbecue, he should break its neck instead." He gave the nape of Layla's neck a playful pinch and grinned.

"Will you shut up and get your head out of your ass for a minute?" she said. "Where is he?" It occurred to her that Ethan still had the knife. The twins' dad was packing up the last of their camping gear in the back of the Subaru. *Hurry up, get out of here*, she thought.

"He's sitting in the pine trees." The rabbit tried to crawl over Will's shoulder. "Pretty mad that he didn't get away with it, I guess."

Layla headed into the grove. She found Ethan sitting on a carpet of needles, carving patterns in the dirt. He didn't look up when she stopped before him.

"Give me that," she said, extending her hand but readying her muscles in case of an attack. In the woods the sunlit leaves and insect noises crystallized, as if she were on drugs. She remembered the first time she smoked pot in high school, she and a boyfriend alone behind her house; the woods had turned all glassy and sharp, like now.

Ethan didn't move. Her body trembled all the way through her feet to the spongy ground. But at least he was below her, cross-legged. "Whose knife is that?" she asked.

"Will's," he answered quietly. "I'm going to give it back to him."

She inched her hand closer. "I'll make sure Will gets it."

He clamped the Swiss Army shut and raised it without looking up at her. So much for her idea that Will might be a good influence, but then she couldn't blame the cousins for being country boys. She pocketed the knife.

Ethan sprang to his feet, not bothering to shake off the needles and dirt clinging to his shorts. At full height, he surpassed her by a mere two inches, but the rest of his frame had filled out lately; he was fast becoming a man. Layla stood a petite five-foot-four. One shove would send her reeling. "Just a minute," she called. Now that she had the knife, she grabbed his shoulder as he brushed past, pressed her nails in. "That rabbit needs to go back to wherever you got him from."

"He doesn't belong anywhere. I bought him," he retorted.

"That's not a pet store bunny."

He spun around. "I know he's not! Will picked me up, we stopped by his friend's house, and their family raises them. So I got one."

"You stole it?"

"I didn't steal it. He's got a bad eye, they can't show him. So I got a deal." Ethan's face puffed red underneath his tan. He breathed heavily, nostrils flared. "Ask Will," he said. "He'll tell you."

Through the pines, the swimming beach stood deserted, except for Will and Barbecue. The rabbit now nestled in Will's arms, a mass of dense fur.

Ethan sauntered ahead, drawing his slender, sinewy arm through the cattails along the shore like a blade. Layla quickened her pace to catch up with him. "Why are you doing this?" she demanded.

"Because you're weak," he replied, staring ahead.

"What?"

"You heard me," he said. "Dad used to call you weak and he's right." Ethan glanced from her to Will, then back to her, adding, "You're disgusting." He sprinted toward the odor of sizzling meat and firecracker smoke at the main camp.

Layla fell in step with Will. The rabbit's head bobbed up and down in the crook of his arm with every jouncing step. "Give him to me," she said. She didn't know where she would put a rabbit for the night, but she wanted to take care of him until she could figure out what to do. Maybe spread some newspapers out in the kitchen, get out the old toddler fence. She bent down for a better look.

Barbecue blinked and stared ahead with two ruby-rimmed, perfect eyes.

•

The new house needed quite a bit of work. For the last couple of weeks, Will had been helping Layla turn the place into a home. This evening, Layla and Will worked on assembling the porch furniture while Ethan was holed up in his room. He hadn't come out since morning, when Layla discovered he'd wet the bed, something he hadn't done since the long ordeal of his father's highly publicized trial. When Layla had offered to wash the sheets, he swatted her away and slammed the door in her face.

Through the screened kitchen door, Layla eyed Barbecue, his fur pressed against the lattice of the toddler gate. She could just make out the twitch of his nose. "I don't know what I'm going to do with him," she said.

"He's a good kid," Will said. "He'll always be a good kid."

"I meant the rabbit."

Will stepped closer, leaned across the screen to look. He smelled strongly of tanned skin and the greased metal of tools, and she realized how void her life had become of a vibrant, hopeful male presence. While Ethan was at KidsPeace, she'd gone on some dates but nothing lasting. She missed sex.

"Yeah, I thought you'd have gotten rid of him right away," Will said.

"I suppose I will soon," she said. "But I could use a friend."

"Even one who can't talk back?" he replied.

Barbecue rose on his hind legs, chin lifted, looking around as if contemplating life on the other side. Several times since his arrival she had lifted the rabbit to eye-level, as if he were a baby, and stared at him. Once she had pressed him to her chest and roamed the house, searching for something, she didn't know what. But as much as she liked keeping him around, piss-soaked newspapers and tiny pellets of shit were not part of the landscape Layla had envisioned for her new home.

"Would you take the bunny?" she asked. Will's family had raised deer as a side business for years; his father had a fondness for animals and plenty of pens.

"He'd make a nice barbecue, it's true," Will said.

She let out a groan. "Until we can figure out what to do with him."

Will touched her shoulder in a way that made her grow hot. "Sure," he said.

Later, when she mulled over what happened, she couldn't remember who started the kiss, but she hoped it had been him. For a minute all she tasted was his mouth, sweet from the cherry soda he'd been drinking. Their damp, warm t-shirts rubbed against one another. With each breath she inhaled the scent of insect repellent mixed with the faintness of her nephew's cologne and pulled away when she recognized that it was the same kind she bought for Ethan. Finally she reached inside her shirt and straightened her bra straps. "I'm thirty-eight," she said. "That's more than twice your age."

"I can do math," he said. He picked up the drill and kept his grin fixed on her. "Pretty good at it, too. Engineering major, remember?" He spurted two whirls out of the drill.

She laughed, shaking her head, and picked up the next piece of furniture. The buzz of the drill poured through the silence between them, and the night air pressed cool at their backs.

When they were finished, Layla invited Will inside for a beer as a reward for his help. Ethan leaned back at the table, drinking a glass of milk. In his lap sat Barbecue, and he stroked the pet absently. Layla's stomach dropped. Had Ethan seen what had happened between them?

"Thought you didn't like rabbits," Will said.

"You know I wasn't going to waste him," Ethan mumbled.

Layla opened the beers. "Will's going to take Barbecue for a while."

"That's fine," Ethan said. "I can't expect either of you to care about what I think, anyway. You're obviously too busy fucking each other."

She shook her head, saying, "Nothing like that has happened."

"You're being a punk," Will said, eyes narrowing, "Apologize."

"Nobody cares what I think." Ethan drained the rest of his milk. "Just keep out of my way."

Layla wanted to reach across the table and slap him, if slapping would have done any good.

"You and Dad both thought I was totally oblivious, but I knew everything," Ethan said. "Your little agreement before you split."

At this she said nothing, clasped her hands together and stared at her engagement ring with quivering lips. Why did she still wear that ring? It captured a time forever untarnished: she and Greg blasting down the highway in his parents' old TR6, the promise that one day she might again feel nothing but the wind in her hair.

When she looked up, Ethan was wiping his eyes on his sweatshirt sleeve. He said, sniffling, "What? I'm sick of you ignoring me."

Will's eyes danced over them both. He took an eager sip from his beer.

"You think your panty-dropping will make some guy stay, but it won't," Ethan said to her. "You don't know how to love anyone." When he stood up, Layla reached for his shoulder, but Ethan shrugged her off with a hard elbow to the collarbone.

Will darted forward, in a second wedged between them. By then Ethan was slugging away. He stood nearly as tall as his older cousin, and the two slammed against the counter, cupboards rattling. Layla tried to pull them apart, but Ethan kicked her hard in the shin, told her to fuck off. The two backed against the table and Ethan's fingers struggled for the tall milk glass before Layla grabbed it out of the way just in time. In the scuffle they knocked over the rabbit pen, and Barbecue peeled off into the dark living room.

She called the police and the KidsPeace emergency line taped on the fridge. Will finally pinned his cousin against the wall. Both boys panted; Ethan writhed and hurled insults. Layla fled, her shin pulsing and already starting to bruise. She limped through the downstairs rooms, straining for any flashes of white in the shadowed corners, behind the couches, searched for the pair of ruby-glowing eyes, until the police arrived, followed by the KidsPeace van. After the police questioning, the KidsPeace workers restrained Ethan in a straitjacket. Layla couldn't see through the long swinging bangs that hid her son's eyes. She had been too afraid to take him for a haircut; what if he wrestled the scissors from the barber? Would she have to live in fear of what her son might do for the rest of her life? As they escorted Ethan past Layla, she saw lines of tears in the hallway light, running out from under the bangs and down her boy's neck.

•

Together, Layla and Will combed the downstairs for Barbecue. With most of the house in a state of unpacking flux, nooks abounded for a terrified rabbit to hide. Finally they found him in the room designated for her home office, where he had squeezed behind a stand of potted plants. She gave the rabbit a long hug and then handed him reluctantly to Will. As soon as her nephew's truck backed down the driveway, she set about cleaning up the damage in the kitchen, crying the whole time.

Later on, in the bedroom mirror, she studied herself. Her legs had lost some tone, but she still had a good body—no stomach, no flabbiness to her arms. She never let a day pass without polish on her toes. Every six weeks she spruced up her color to its original blonde, now dubbed "Indian Summer." Pulling her hair back, she peered closer to examine her face. Will had certainly found her attractive, hadn't he? As soon as the smile broke across her face, she sank back to the bed.

Then she thought of Ethan's father, Greg. Will's family visited him every few months and insisted that in the two years he'd been in prison, he'd changed for the better. She would prefer not involving Greg, but maybe he would have some kind of positive impact. Neither she nor Ethan could afford another big mistake, but what choices did she have left?

•

Ethan remained at KidsPeace for another two weeks. Meanwhile, Layla wrote to Greg to arrange a visit. "We might even have the visiting room to ourselves," Greg said eagerly when he'd called her collect. She told him about the rabbit incident and the fight with Will. "No matter what the counselors say, we're still his parents," Greg said. "We have every right to decide on a visit."

She avoided Will until he called to report that Barbecue had adjusted well to the wooden cage he'd built. "You should stop by and check it out," he said.

"I'm busy," she said. "I'm taking Ethan to visit Greg."

"You are? Let me come with you."

"I don't think that's a good idea right now," she said. "Ethan doesn't know we're going."

When Layla signed Ethan out of KidsPeace she said nothing. She just led him to the car and took the other ramp on the highway. When he demanded an answer, she told him, "You'll see."

It was a five-hour drive to Huntingdon State Prison, but Layla kept the car at a steady speed, too fast for Ethan to jump out. Far from the crowded eastern part of the state, the farms and golden cornfields grew more abundant amidst the green, jutting hills, and she had forgotten how quickly the remoteness expanded near State College. Such isolation, especially in winter, would be punishment in itself.

Groggy from the sedatives he'd been given earlier, Ethan fumed and cursed. "All of this is your fault," he said. "You never put out enough, that's why Dad wanted a divorce. I heard him say so all the time to his friends."

After so many years of marriage, I'm recouping my losses.

Those were Greg's exact words. So he and Layla made their agreement, but she never imagined Ethan would walk in on Greg having sex with a twenty-year-old stripper from Spanky's East named Barb.

She turned to Ethan, hunched in the passenger seat. "What does that have to do with what you almost did to the rabbit?" she asked.

He didn't answer.

"It's called an open marriage," she said. "Obviously, it failed on several levels."

Ethan leaned back, arms crossed, and closed his eyes. "Don't lie. If you could do it all over again, you would. 'Hey, Honey, let's save our marriage by bringing strangers home to fuck.'"

She said, "All I can do now is ask you to forgive me. Okay?"

She guessed Ethan must have seen a lot she didn't even know about, during the weekends Greg had custody of him in the years between the divorce and his arrest. She remembered her disappointment when she heard Greg, with his brilliant mind, was hanging out at strip clubs with younger lab techs from the pharmaceutical company where he'd worked for seventeen years. How many women did he parade in front of their son?

When Ethan had delivered a designer handbag to her as a birthday present, she questioned its origins. Greg had told her about a business venture with some of his friends from the lab, but she didn't care to ask any more about it. A year and a half later, a SWAT team burst into their old house while Ethan was staying for the weekend. They arrested Greg and charged him with drug manufacturing and running a criminal organization. The DEA found a hidden lab chock full of chemicals, one of the biggest methamphetamine operations ever seized on the East coast. They dragged Ethan out of bed and questioned him for hours.

Now, as Layla wound through the last of the big hills and descended upon the town, she spotted the prison. Ethan had been drifting in and out of naps and spotted the Huntingdon road sign as they exited the highway. "No fucking way," he muttered. An intersection loomed at the bottom of the ramp, and the car grated to a halt. He squeezed the door handle.

"Go ahead," she said. "Look around. Where are you going to run, the woods? This town *is* the prison."

His hand dropped to his lap.

The barbs curved like devilish nails and the wire gleamed as Layla drove along the stretch of winding road. The prison was a looming, walled Victorian fortress, the red of its bricks having long ago faded to a rusty grey. Armed guards perched atop its turrets. She pulled into the visitor's lot next to a few middle-aged corrections officers talking on motorcycles. They dismounted and looked like identical caricatures, their sausage limbs stuffed in uniforms, seams ready to burst. They marched in the opposite direction, chins up, arms swinging with wide haughty steps.

"I hate you," Ethan said. "And I'm not seeing him."

Layla thought quickly. "You're on the list," she said. "You have to come in. I have your birth certificate and everything. You don't think the prison just lets unidentified visitors hang around outside for a few hours, huh?"

The visiting room was just a few shabby seating areas and ancient vending machines. She sat on one of the dingy cushioned chairs and watched out the window for Greg to appear on the walk. Ethan fought with a battered machine until it spat out a bag of nuts and a candy bar.

Layla spotted her ex-husband, tiny at first, in a maroon suit and unescorted on the path, his gait jaunty and brisk. As he got closer she saw his face had thinned, but he wore a big smile. He entered and squeezed Ethan so hard that the boy's feet swung off the ground. Ethan refused to hug him back. Instead his son hung in his arms like a flopped-over scarecrow. "What's this?" Greg asked, his voice like gravel.

Layla gave Greg an awkward hug. His muscles were taut underneath the jumpsuit, and the veins bulged in his neck.

For a moment all three of them sat in silence, the air stuffy despite the open windows; outside, the panorama of fields and mountains snapped to stillness, as if the world had stopped.

Well, here we are, Layla thought. *What happens now?*

"How's the rabbit?" Greg asked.

"Barbecue's just fine," she said. "I've been meaning to stop by and check on him."

Greg chuckled. "Wait, you've got to be kidding me. The rabbit's name is Barbecue?"

"I named him," Ethan said, arms crossed.

"And you haven't come up with another name?"

"Barbecue was the perfect name," Ethan said.

"Okay, okay, I'm sorry." Greg cleared his throat. "I've been somewhat sheltered, you could say." He reached for Ethan's candy bar and began to scarf it down.

"It's not funny," Layla said. She pictured Barbecue sitting pertly on his haunches in the kitchen corner.

"Mom's fucking Will," Ethan said.

"Who?" Greg said, choking on a bite of peanuts and caramel.

"Will, my cousin. *Your* nephew."

"That's not true," Layla said, shaking her head.

"Asshole," Ethan said to her.

Greg grabbed Ethan's arm.

Ethan's chin drooped to his chest and his eyes hid behind his bangs. "I want you to have not done what you did," he said. "But that's impossible."

"I'm sorry for all of it, Ethan," Greg replied. "So is your mom."

Ethan didn't answer. Layla quietly wept and Greg reached for her hand. After a long silence, she promised they'd visit again soon.

On the way home, Layla and Ethan stopped to eat at a Denny's. She made him take his sedative with the meal. Ethan didn't touch his plate but for the pill he'd wrapped in a piece of pancake and washed down with a glass of milk. At the prison, Greg had mentioned an alternate route he'd discovered while assigned to a road crew, and Layla debated whether she should take the highway home or the scenic back roads through the farmland of Happy Valley.

•

Faint pinks and yellows fired the sky around eight o'clock when Layla's tires crunched onto Will's parents' driveway. Ethan stayed in the car while she walked around to the back of the house. Will was erecting some wire fencing, part of the deer run that extended up the forested hillside. Barbecue hopped around in an unpainted pen made out of two-by-fours and chicken wire. Will didn't say anything, just absently swung his hammer. "I know this sounds silly," Layla said, blushing, "but I really want the rabbit home tonight."

Will said he'd bring it over in his truck that evening and set up the pen for her.

Back home, Ethan ignored Layla's request that he help them move the pen and stole upstairs. Layla shut Barbecue in the laundry room, then joined Will at the truck bed. "You think he'll try and mess with the rabbit again?" Will asked. He set down his corner of the pen near the porch steps. "In that case, I'd rather keep Barbecue with us."

"He's the only thing that calms me down," she answered, stopping herself before she said, *from Ethan*. "You don't want to stay overnight, do you? I'm pretty edgy. Ethan didn't say much the whole ride back."

"Not really," he said. "But I guess I could."

"I'll make up the couch," she said.

They slipped inside. Even in the twilight, she could detect his muscles rippling underneath his shirt. She gathered Barbecue from the laundry basket and cuddled him to her neck; kissing his pink nose, she smiled. Tomorrow she would slice up some apples and carrots for his dish. She carried the rabbit upstairs and paused by Ethan's closed door but heard nothing; the crack under his door remained dark. In her bedroom she watched a comedy show, the rabbit perched in her lap. The downstairs shower sputtered to life—Will, she thought, cleaning up before bed. After an hour of laughing and scratching the rabbit behind the ears, she finally felt relaxed enough to sleep. She returned Barbecue to his pen and left a dim porch light on for him.

On her way through the house, Will stirred under his sheet and mumbled something in his sleep. She told him to go back to sleep, but he sat up on his elbow and squinted at her, half-awake. She padded to the couch, leaned over, and spoke again in a hushed voice. He raised a hand and slowly skimmed it across her breasts. Layla caught her breath. Will's warm palm rested on her skin, then his arm fell back to his side. She hovered for a few moments, unable to move until she was quite sure he was sleeping.

Layla retreated upstairs to bed and touched herself,

fantasizing about the alternate outcome—that Will had been awake, that they kissed like the other night, only this time their clothes came off, and she wasn't alone and almost forty years old. Afterward, she lay still in her bed with only emptiness to embrace. In the morning she would tell Will he could no longer spend time at her house, no matter what. No more blundering through the same mistakes. She loved her son too much. Love was endless forgiveness, and she would love Ethan even when his behavior least deserved it. Even if he never forgave her.

·

In the middle of the night Layla awoke twice. The first time she heard a shrieking like animals mating—the neighbors' cats most likely. She sank back to a deep sleep. But then the downstairs smoke alarm went off and she jerked awake, heart thudding like a brick. The air smelled faintly of smoke. She thought of Will—why hadn't he roused her? The sound of footsteps muffled by ripping cardboard floated up the stairwell.

She seized her phone as she hurried for the stairs. Smoke and an odor like burning hair swirled up from the first floor. At the landing the living room scene came fully into view. She clutched the wall.

Ethan, nude except for his cotton briefs, had kindled a fire in the middle of the half-furnished room. He knelt with his back toward her, feeding the flames with broken packing materials: torn-up boxes and balls of newspaper. Barbecue roasted in the blaze, his fur a patchwork of black gluey tufts in some places; in others only bare, charred skin remained.

From her position she couldn't see over the back of the couch. She sank slowly to her knees and groped the phone, hoping Will had fled. All she could mumble to the emergency operator was the address before she lost the connection. Possibly they would dismiss it as just a prank by some teenagers.

But she couldn't just wait there. She climbed to her feet, threw on the overhead light switch. By the time she descended to the last step, Ethan had twisted around. She crept to the couch and froze, the fire leaping up from the floor, heat smacking her skin. Its glare made spots appear and her eyes watered from the thickening haze. But her vision was still clear enough that she cried out at the glint of the kitchen knife in her son's outstretched hand, the blade now rushing toward her.

Uninvited Guests

The Reverend refused to rent his carriage house apartment to unmarried females who "entertained any male guest other than kin." Nancy would never have agreed to such staunch, ridiculous terms, but she had her three-month-old daughter to consider. The baby's father was in prison for beating Nancy at the end of her second trimester, and her own mother lived in a non-air-conditioned apartment in a dilapidated Victorian up in Sanford. If Nancy didn't take the Reverend's offer, her next step would be the women's shelter in downtown Orlando. At that point, social services wouldn't waste too much time in taking away her baby. With that on her mind, Nancy accepted the Reverend's rental and verbally agreed to his terms.

One day after she'd been settled in for a week, the Reverend's 1989 Town and Country ambled down the shady driveway and came to a rest in front of the carriage house, below the second story apartment where Nancy was swaying in the frayed porch hammock, crying. She swung her feet to the floor when she heard the crunch of her landlord's oxfords on the gravel, wiped her tears and quickly rubbed her wet palms on her pants.

The Reverend skipped up the stairs. His slight frame gave

him a youthful demeanor in spite of his salt-and-pepper hair and mustache.

"Thought I'd give you a courtesy call," he said. "Kate"—that was his peachy-skinned wife—"mentioned that she saw some fellas in a pickup come back here and drop you off not long ago."

"My co-workers," Nancy replied. She pretended to brush some crumbs off her shirt. "The Parks and Rec guys said they'd give me a ride home every day for lunch. Since we work so close by."

"I guessed as much," the Reverend said. He stuck both hands onto his hips. "But Kate's more than happy to fix you lunch regularly."

"That's nice of you," she said. "I'll think about it."

He stood there, bouncing on the balls of his feet a few times as if he was summoning energy. "What I'm saying is," he said, and his voice had turned quiet. "No strange men are permitted on my property."

"But they're my co-workers," she said, stiffening. "Not one of them even set foot onto the driveway. They're not 'guests.'" A nervous laugh escaped her.

"To me they are," he snapped. "Uninvited guests. Only takes one of them to make trouble. Are they locals? From Eatonville?"

"They're Haitian," she answered.

The Reverend shook his head, traced his button-down shirt where it covered his hard stomach. "You realize this is not only for your own safety, but my wife's and mine?" he asked. "Mind you, I get the distinct impression you're not used to a caring father-figure looking out for your best interest."

She didn't say anything. He said he hoped she'd had a nice lunch and left.

Nancy watched him cross the backyard and disappear into

his house. The two-story colonial needed a new coat of white paint. A statue of an angel kneeling in prayer tilted on shaded, uneven ground. American flags of all sizes draped every post from the porch railings to the mailbox. She had agreed to the wife, Kate, minding her daughter because the Reverend had made an offer at a fraction of the regular day-care cost. Kate's fussing over the couple's bull terrier irked Nancy, how every Friday afternoon, fresh from the groomer's, the dog yapped incessantly as Nancy arrived home from work. Sometimes, if pet and owner were on the porch, Kate would scoop up the creature, bow sticking out from its collar, and watch as Nancy parked. The image of the Reverend's dog-coddling spouse spooning her daughter full of homemade applesauce while Nancy spent her days unlocking and locking park gates and checking swing-sets once again spurred her tears.

•

The next morning, Nancy played with the baby in the side yard on a bunny quilt loaned by Kate. The Reverend busied himself with yard chores, but Nancy had the distinct feeling he was spying. He'd been straightening that sagging bougainvillea trellis for the last forty-five minutes.

She scooped up her daughter, tugged the baby's bonnet further down over her black fuzzy ringlets, and strolled over to the Reverend. The sun blazed the yard. The Reverend had already spent several late morning hours scurrying and fiddling outdoors. His heavily applied Old Spice startled her even more than usual.

"I'm going to have my co-workers drop me off at the end of the driveway when I come home for lunch from now on," she said. "If that's okay with you."

His slender, hairless fingers gripped the white edges of the trellis. "That's fine," he said. "But I still don't quite understand why you wouldn't want to put your feet up in our kitchen and visit with your baby girl while you've got the time."

Because that's the only goddamned hour I get for myself, she screamed inside. Tight-lipped, she said, "Thanks. But it's enough that your wife watches her."

"You got somebody coming by here soon?" he asked. "Normally we head up to the shop at eleven-thirty, but I want to make sure I can lend a hand."

"He should be here any minute," she said. Her daughter squirmed and her tiny, tan fingers groped Nancy's neck.

The Reverend removed his sunglasses and polished them with the end of his shirt. He squinted at Nancy and asked, "Where's your baby's daddy?"

She answered, "In Iraq."

"A serviceman!" he exclaimed. "Kate bakes sugar cookies for each holiday and sends them to the troops. You be sure and give her your man's address."

"We're getting a divorce," she added quickly.

Kate breezed out the front door, towards the car.

"Now we know the story," the Reverend said. He thudded his palm against his forehead and waved at his wife, grinning. In the passenger seat, Kate's strawberry-red bob grazed her shoulders. He headed for the car, saying over his shoulder, "We were hoping you weren't one of these poor girls who let themselves be victimized by passion."

"Don't have much time for that," she replied. Which was true, lately. She shifted the baby to her other side, taking the pressure off her arm. The fracture had healed, but the bone remained weak from her ex's farewell.

"A crime of passion's a crime just like any other," the

Reverend said, and climbed into the driver's seat.

Nancy stood there frozen, her underarms damp and her daughter solid against her ribs. She squinted and looked back at the carriage house framed by Spanish moss, her front porch directly across from the Reverend's bedroom windows. A man like her ex would sneak past the drooping wooden fence along the driveway, no problem—luckily he was locked up in the state pen and not getting out anytime soon. He hadn't once looked at her in court, with her bruises and belly; she hadn't sent him pictures of their daughter. She pictured him now, alone and memorizing the walls of his cell.

A pickup with oversized tires rolled up underneath the oaks and parked facing the bug-eyed Town and Country. Reggae music radiated out of the open windows, and Bobby waved a hello. He'd brought the last of Nancy's second-hand furniture from her mom's house.

The Reverend pulled out alongside the truck. "Cousin Bobby," he called with a curt nod.

Neither Nancy nor Bobby moved until the Town and Country disappeared down the road. She watched the vehicle as it braked for a half-second at the stop sign at the end of the block. The Reverend's license plate read, "Acts 22:16." He turned left and was off to his Bible bookstore in Apopka. She would have to look up the verse later; no doubt the Reverend would have a Bible stashed in some dusty drawer of her rental. Had either he or his wife ever known any passion?

Nancy circled the truck to greet her cousin. She tried to explain the Reverend's rules to Bobby, who just laughed. She asked about his friend she'd met a couple weeks ago, the one with the big cauliflower nose named Heath. She had met up with them at a bar in downtown Deland after the two had gone skydiving for Heath's thirtieth birthday. Bobby obsessed over the experience and raved about becoming an instructor, while Heath wrote down reasons habitual skydiving was a bad idea on napkins and coasters. The end count came to thirty-three. Heath stuffed the lists underneath Bobby's shirt. All except for one Nancy had saved.

After Bobby left, she used the key hidden in back of the angel statue to slip into the main house. An oversized, gold-embossed family Bible was displayed on an oak stand in the foyer. The pages smelled like old wallpaper, as if the book had gotten wet and spoiled, then dried.

Acts 22:16 read: "And now what are you waiting for? Get up, be baptized and wash your sins away, calling on his name."

She read it a few times, but she didn't believe in sin. Not even after everything that had happened to her, all the blood. Was she supposed to believe her beautiful daughter came from someplace as small and weak as sin? Is that what the Reverend wanted her to believe? Maybe his remark about passion was right, but only partly. She wanted passion and she wanted love, too. Together, like the bright, climbing bougainvillea intertwined on the arching trellis.

·

When the Reverend and Kate returned home in the late afternoon, the Reverend had changed into a crisp American flag button-down, cowboy boots, and rather snug-fitting jeans. He watered the potted palms resting in the late afternoon shade of the carriage house for half an hour before he and Kate rapped on Nancy's door and invited her to join them for dinner at Bubbalou's Bar-B-Que. Nancy's daughter awoke from her nap and began wailing, so she declined. Kate mentioned that she and the Reverend would be going to a 4th of July fireworks show and wouldn't arrive home until late.

That evening, Bobby called Nancy and asked if he could swing by again with Heath. Nancy told the boys to come on over.

•

Bobby and Heath showed up with two six packs of Corona, a camping grill, and marshmallows, and hastily found some sticks for roasting. Soon the humid air filled with the smell of sweet, burnt sugar. The baby cooed and kicked in her carrier seat, her dark brown eyes fixated on the glowing embers.

Heath had been working in his family's orange groves all day, so that his enormous nose, now sunburned, startled Nancy even more than the first time they'd met. She had to force herself not to stare at the almost-deformed, strawberry-hued monstrosity. Even the pores resembled the seedy exterior of the fruit. "You like roasted cherry tomatoes? Cause I got one right here," he joked, and the three burst out laughing.

Nancy brought up the night in Deland, post-skydiving.

"Don't remember much about that night," Heath said. "I don't think I felt the ground underneath my feet for about five days after that."

"You don't remember this?" She rooted around in her purse for the napkin containing part of his list. But by the time she produced it, the boys were in another fierce debate about skydiving.

"I'm going again, end of this week," Bobby said, grinning.

"You're only into this because you don't have a girlfriend," Heath countered. "Number one, a woman with any sense wouldn't let you jump out of a plane every day, and number two you wouldn't want to if you were in love. Right, Nancy?"

She shrugged. "I've never seen Bobby so excited about something."

"Wait a minute," Heath said, jumping up. He rifled through his pockets and the marshmallow bag, then ran out to the truck. When he returned he pressed a tiny orange into Nancy's hand and said, "It's one of those inflatable things that you stick in water, and over a couple of days it grows. My folks have an orange stand in Maitland and we sell them there. They're called 'Passionfruits.' Kind of silly, but each one's got a different love saying once it gets full size."

She rolled the orange around in her palm. "But I have to wait a few days for the message?" she asked.

"Just a little gift," Heath replied. He shoved his hands in his belt loops and looked down. Then he grabbed the tiny orange from her and plunked it into his plastic cup of Corona. "Let's see if beer makes it grow any faster."

She laughed.

Several hours passed. After nightfall, Heath rested his freckled wrist on Nancy's knee as he rotated his marshmallow stick, and every once in awhile she reached down to touch her daughter in the carrier seat.

When the Town and Country quaked into its worn spot beneath the dangling moss, Nancy squirmed. The couple had to be in their sixties, at least; surely they were exhausted from their pork platters, hush puppies, and fireworks, and wouldn't rush back to the carriage house to investigate further. Besides, the Reverend knew Bobby's truck from that morning.

After a few minutes of the bull terrier yapping hello to its owners, the porch light at the main house went out. Heath's fingers trailed over her knee.

They're in for the night, thank God, Nancy thought. She snuggled in closer to Heath.

Though it was only ten-thirty, the guys decided to leave.

They were supposed to meet up with some friends in Lake Helen who had illegal fireworks, the kind that someone needed a license to shoot off.

As Bobby put out the grill, Nancy spotted the flashlight beaming across the yard. The light reached the bottom of her steps and the bull terrier's nails scratched the wood, his panting interspersed with sneezes. The dog and Reverend popped up out of the shadows.

"Good evening," Nancy said loudly. The boys echoed her greeting and plunked their beers at their feet.

"What are these two doing here?" the Reverend asked, bounding forward. The bull terrier barked without cease and darted around the young men's legs. Nancy caught Heath's mystified face as the Reverend skimmed the light over him, illuminating the nose. Its bumpiness extended every which way so that smaller noses seemed to be taking root in the middle of his face.

"Just enjoying the evening, sir," Heath said, puffing out his chest. "You and your wife have a nice time?"

"Kate won't go to sleep until these two uninvited guests move off the property," the Reverend replied. "Police station's just a couple of blocks over."

Bobby grabbed the grill and it scraped across the planks. Heath stooped to retrieve his beer; with the other hand he pulled his keys out of his pocket and jangled them. Nancy hadn't even exchanged numbers with him yet.

"I'm twenty-six years old, Reverend," she said, stepping closer to Heath, the flashlight still shining on his sunburned nose, the rest of him pale in comparison. She pinched his shirt. "This is my husband, just got back from Iraq."

For a moment she hoped for the Reverend's flashlight to clatter to the ground. The boys kept silent and didn't move.

"I owe you all my deepest apologies," the Reverend said. He pressed his fist to his lips, shaking his head. Then he stepped forward and gripped Heath's hand so hard the young man coughed a little. "God bless you for your service." The Reverend sniffed as if he might cry. "Kate and I couldn't be more—well, now I'd better go. Didn't mean to interrupt." He released Heath's hand as quickly as he'd snatched it and hurried to the steps, bull terrier at his heels.

"Thanks," Heath said to her, and then to Bobby, "You still want to run up to Lake Helen, shoot off those fireworks? It's an awfully long ride. Cops'll be everywhere tonight."

"Happy Fourth of July!" the Reverend crowed from the yard.

Nancy plucked a lukewarm marshmallow off a stick and ate it.

•

Bobby fell asleep on the couch. After alternating bouts of kissing and shoving away hands, Heath finally dozed in bed beside Nancy. But he snored and kept her awake so that she got to thinking about the confrontation with the Reverend that evening. She recalled the Bible verse that he paraded on his license plate, and while she didn't care for the last part she liked the beginning: "And now what are you waiting for? Get up." What was she waiting for? She left the hot bed to check her sleeping daughter.

She saw only two options: to struggle on her own, slapping away others; or to gather help from every source to give her daughter a chance at a decent life, like the blooming bougainvillea vine using the rickety but upright trellis to grow. It occurred to her that passion might not come in the form of a man.

•

In the week that followed, the tiny orange, Heath's gift to Nancy, had plumped up to the size of a fist and finally spouted its message: "Orange you going to love me?" Kate prepared lunch for Nancy each day and offered to watch the baby one evening when Heath invited Nancy on a date. He stayed the night without interruption.

On Sunday, Nancy walked to the corner store to buy a newspaper and breakfast ingredients to surprise Heath. Now that his sunburn had subsided, his cauliflower nose appeared smaller and less bulbous. When she returned, the Reverend and his wife were clipping down the front path to the Town and Country. Kate wore Capri pants, sandals and a straw hat, the Reverend a grey suit and alligator dress shoes. A Bible stuck out from underneath his arm. All three exchanged good mornings. "Have a good sermon for today?" Nancy asked.

"We have several baptisms," he said, shooting her a knowing glance as he opened the car door for his wife. "And *they* always take center stage. People love to see sins washed away. Especially when they're somebody else's."

Nancy walked on with her purchases.

"Sure glad to see you two are sticking it out," the Reverend called. His car door slammed.

She froze for a moment before turning around. "We're not sure yet," she said. "Just taking it slow."

"We've been praying for you," he answered. Beside him Kate nodded a silent yes as she stared blankly ahead. He said, "We lost our daughter to a mixed up man. You remind us a lot of her." He faced forward then, and the long body of the Town and Country rolled onto the road and sailed away.

Nancy continued, the driveway already warm underneath

her soles, the midmorning heat relentless. A sunbeam struck one half of the angel. From the carriage house her daughter cried, and Nancy hurried underneath the sprawling bougainvillea.

The Lung

A dozen years ago, the doctors took my lung. I didn't tell my girlfriend, Margot, until just the other day because I was sure she would break up with me. I still smoke (cigarettes and weed), and she hates these habits in general. Now she's worried the remaining lung will suffer the same fate, that if I don't stop soon, "it's just a matter of time." But I quit trying to quit a long time ago and would rather spend what's left enjoying life.

One day Margot and I are lounging around my pool after lunch and she asks if a friend can stop by. So I say, sure, why not? I should have known something was up. Her friend is an acupuncturist. Before I know it I'm confined beneath an umbrella and have to keep still. Needles parade across my body. I try to relax but keep eyeing my cigarettes and lighter on the table next to me. Just sliding a smoke out of the pack is practically impossible with that many needles on the back of my hand. So instead I pick up the half a joint sitting in the ashtray which, a few moments earlier, the acupuncturist and I were passing back and forth.

In the pool Margot shimmies off the blow-up mattress and wades to the side closest to me. "You light that up, I'm leaving," she says.

But I light up. "There's no reason to worry about my lung," I say, taking two tiny puffs. "Besides, smoking had nothing to do with my illness. They ran tests. I had some sort of weird, rare genetic cancer."

"Oh, sure," she says. "Of course you did." She emerges all curvy and dripping.

I don't say anything. I tilt my head back and suck in a nice, long drag just for spite. But then I think about if Margot does leave for good, the house empty of our laughter.

"And what if I try to quit but still can't?" I ask. "Does that mean I love you any less?"

"Do you love me?" she asks. "I wonder how you can claim that, when you obviously don't care very much about your health."

I stub out the joint.

Margot drifts to the outdoor shower. As I sit there covered in needles, the acupuncturist dozing in the chair beside me, I watch her soap and rinse through the shrubbery. When Margot comes out her face is wet, but her eyes are ember-red, either from the chlorine or maybe tears. And I'm troubled by this because as much as I seek to enjoy every moment with Margot, I want just as much for her to enjoy me, too—otherwise, what's the point? I fought the cancer after my divorce, by myself. I wouldn't want to go through that alone again.

•

The next morning we awake to the smell of smoke. A haze hangs outside even though the night before was clear. The local news tells us that wildfires are burning across the state. I'm glued to the TV most of the morning.

I work in the field of environmental protection, although the staff under my management amends developers' agreements, not forest fires. A storm out in the Atlantic is blowing winds south, trapping the worst of the smoke right above Central Florida. The reporter concludes by warning that anyone with breathing conditions should spend the day indoors.

I step onto the patio and light my usual morning cigarette. Any smoker will tell you there's a vast difference between *having* a cigarette and *breathing* smoke. But in a few minutes, the double-inhalation of toxic fumes proves too much and I'm clutching my sides in a coughing fit.

Margot waltzes out with our coffee and the *Sentinel*. She says nothing about my hacking spell, but shoves the ashtray at me so hard that it wobbles on its rim like a hubcap before coming to rest.

"My lung works at eighty-five percent capacity," I start. "That's better than most people with two lungs."

"You're a coward," she says.

"If that's how you see it," I say. "I try every day not to smoke."

"You say you love me and want a long, passionate life together," she says, "yet you act to destroy that very possibility every time you bring one of those cancer sticks to your lips. Either you want to live, or you want to smoke and die young. Which is the truth?"

Margot is a lawyer, and for the first time I'm realizing just how she has won her reputation for ruthless cross-examination in the toughest of cases. "Please stay," I say. "See, this is the reason I love you. You're right, and you're the most brilliant woman I've ever known."

"I appreciate that," she says. "But I assure you, I get plenty of praise from my colleagues and everyone else who wants to get in my pants."

She strips off the sarong she wears in the morning, struts over to the pool naked, and dips one foot in the water. Then tugs on her swim cap and plunges into the deep end. I smoke while her egg head skims back and forth over the length of the pool. The yard takes on a dull tinge from the wildfire smoke. Even her cap doesn't gleam its usual bright white.

Then I picture her climbing out, collecting her things, and not coming back. Margot is that type of woman: she won't waste time if she hits an impasse, but will survey her options and hop the next plane to wherever she wants to go. To the extent that I desire her tongue-lashing insights to keep my own ship sailing, I reel back en route.

I fetch my car keys and call out that I'm going to the pharmacy to buy the latest nicotine patch system. I expect her to smile and wave mid-stroke, but she stands up in the shallow end, coughing. She claims the smoky air hurts her eyes and lungs too much. We retreat and barricade ourselves within the air conditioning. I bring her some water, but she is hacking so hard that she runs to the bathroom and throws up.

At the store I buy the most expensive anti-smoking product on the market.

·

By evening the air inside tastes of ash despite our efforts to keep the windows and doors sealed. Margot has an early court case so she spends the night at her house. I go to bed with a burning sore throat and stinging nose. The air is so bad that I can't sleep. I turn on the light and reach for my cure-all remedy (insomnia, nausea, glaucoma)—a joint.

I exhale a lungful and ponder: what's the heart of the trouble between Margot and me? If in order to truly love someone else, you must first completely love yourself, then aren't most relationships not based in love but something else—dependency, security, urgency, sex? But then, if loving yourself includes accepting your own faults and failures, wouldn't that mean the other person has to accept those, too? I check the pulse in my neck, feel the blood gushing through my veins.

I recall my most recent visit to the specialist who removed my lung. We examined my glowing X-rays, and the doctor pointed out the strange starfish arms branching out every-which-way—the solo lung's incredible expansion into the cavity left by its twin.

•

The next evening after dinner, Margot spots the five-step nicotine system and reads the box in its entirety while I stock the dishwasher. "So where'd you stick the patch?" she asks.

"I didn't start yet," I say. "Today was my last day to smoke."

"Oh," she replies, placing the box on the counter as if she had wasted too much time memorizing all those directions and diagrams. Then she rummages through her purse for a piece of dark "antioxidant" chocolate, her nightly habit. Between chews she says, "Are you going to stop smoking weed, too?"

"Weed I can quit anytime," I tell her. "Just whether I want to or not."

She offers me some chocolate, but I refuse. The stuff tastes like dirt pie mixed with soot, not that I would know.

"I love you," she says.

"'I love you,' what does that mean?" I retort, whirling around. "What happens if I quit now but breach contract with a pack of American Spirit in five years? Then you won't quite love me so much, maybe?"

She's quiet for a few moments, collecting her thoughts, and when she speaks her voice is steady, each word deliberately chosen. She says, "I want evidence that you believe in the value of your life, an action or something specific. If not, we might as well end this right now because we'll just keep failing to understand one another."

This argument isn't even about me smoking or having one lung. This is about two people defining what love is going to mean between just them. This is laying a foundation for a brick house rather than plodding along and tossing up some shack of twigs and straw, which is what most people settle for instead. And now the time has come for me to throw down the largest brick of all, the cornerstone upon which my life with Margot will either tower majestically or crumble when the pressure heats up later on. Once again squared off with her brilliant insight, I feel overwhelmingly grateful for her.

"Go into the garage," I say. "Look above the refrigerator in the back. Tell me what you find."

"What does this have to do with anything?" she says. "What am I looking for?"

"A plastic bucket, orange," I say. I flick on the garage light for her.

She returns gagging, but not from the smoke. She carries the sealed bucket far out in front of her with both hands, slides its contents back and forth slightly. The bucket sounds like it has a rock inside as she steps closer to me: *ker-thunk, ker-thunk.*

"Whatever this is, it stinks of chemicals," she says, wrinkling her nose.

"You really don't know?" I ask her. "Look. The bucket's got Xs and crossbones and *cuidado* marked all over it."

"Can I throw this away, please?" she asks.

"Absolutely not," I tell her, pretending to take offense. "That's my lung."

She screams and drops the bucket. It hits the floor but

luckily the hospital must seal up medical waste to outlast a nuclear war because the lid stays on.

"I had to fight with the doctors to let me keep it as a reminder," I say. "Even having that old cancer-ridden thing in my house didn't work to stop me from smoking. And I kept that bucket here and stared at it for a long time, trust me. But that old lung's still here and so am I, and because of that lung I love every moment of my life."

Margot just stands there, one hand plastered over her mouth, staring at me. I stoop down and grasp the bucket.

"Jesus," she mutters. "That's sick."

Ker-thunk, ker-thunk.

But then we both start laughing, and the petrified lung rattles and clunks even more, which makes us crack up even harder. She follows me outside and down the driveway to the trash bin. I throw open the lid and say goodbye to my lung. We wipe our eyes, grip our aching ribs and howl until the smoky air finally turns our chuckles to chokes and we surrender inside to hit the sheets.

•

These days life has shifted somewhat. Instead of having my first cigarette while Margot swims, I join her. Mostly I interfere with her laps by swimming around and groping her naked body, and this begins a cycle of her squirming, crying out in protest and finally, embracing me. She hasn't mentioned my quitting smoking since the night we tossed out my old lung. The wildfires have died down and the wind has shifted, clearing the air. In the late afternoon, the rains come. We make love while the sky pours buckets. Afterward, I sit out back inhaling the clean, cool air brought by the rain and enjoy my only smoke (a post-coital spliff).

One such afternoon Margot slips outside clad in a towel. She prefers the outdoor shower because the indoor one lacks the appeal of geckos and insects darting around her feet, and the slim but sure possibility of a snake. A couple of weeks ago I found a baby rattler while cleaning leaves out of the pool filter. Not what I'd call dangerous or exotic, but Margot likes to pretend we're living our own version of Indiana Jones.

When the shower jerks to life I suddenly feel confessional. Maybe it's the weed. "I was afraid you'd leave," I say. "If I didn't stop smoking."

"Is that why you quit?" she sputters from the shower, but her tone is bemused, sparring. "Mr. I-Don't-Live-In-Fear?"

"Cut it out," I say. "Would you rather I take for granted waking up next to you?"

Eyes closed, head tilted back, her body is framed by the night-blooming jasmine and papaya trees. "*Modus operandi*," she says. "If we love one another, we should use this to keep us in check—that at any time, for any reason, either one of us may leave or die."

"But you're staying?" I ask.

"I'm staying," she says. "And I believe you love me a tad bit more, but that's just today."

I nod and think, fair enough. A great horticulturist accepts that no two days are exactly alike in the natural world, no two moments, no two creatures. That's why living organisms abound with mystery and surprise. I'm fixated by this in Margot, her churning bundle of deliberate yet spontaneous qualities. She's like a reviving serum that keeps me reborn.

Later on, I rummage in my office. The scraping of boxes and groaning of drawers summons Margot. "What are you looking for?" she asks.

"I want you to see my good lung, so you believe me."

She helps me look. Together we tear the desk and filing cabinets apart. We move on to the closet. We conduct this ritual together, unearthing gestures and evidence of my devotions to love and life.

She asks, "How can a lung grow, especially with you smoking?"

"In spite of smoking," I point out. "After the operation, I was still in the hospital but able to walk around, and I went sort of crazy. I did laps around the ward just to prove to myself I was alive. Over and over, all I thought was, 'I have a fantastic lung.'"

Wedged between a stack of bent get-well cards and some back issues of *High Times*, Margot discovers the X-rays. The light is too dim to reveal anything distinct. I turn on the closet light and hold up one sheet of film.

"I don't see anything," she says. "Just a dark blob."

In my hurry to exit the closet, I trip over some boxes. The X-rays fly out of my grasp and fan out across the floor. The afternoon sun hits this side of the house pretty strong when the blinds are wide open.

"Oh, my gosh," she cries. "Is that it?" We both squat near the spread out X-ray sheets. I pick up the transparency on top, walk it over to the window, and stick it inside the frame so that the light shines through.

"Isn't that something," she says, and hugs me from behind.

We study the peculiar image before us. Mysterious as a snowflake, my solo lung has great arms. It splays out in my chest like a flesh-made Star of David and reaches out of my body, across the universe.

Hospice of the Au Pair

Dr. Sam Parkinson was slamming his hips into the groaning au pair, both of them gasping for breath, when he tilted his head and caught his reflection in the skinny mirror hanging on the back of the bathroom door. Grey halos circled his sunken eyes, and spidery red vessels burst across the whites. A voice like that of his thoughts, but not exactly—from somewhere deep and ancient and apart—asked, "Who am I?" He gave the au pair two more pumps, slid out, and collapsed onto the bath mat, still staring into the spotty mirror. But he must have said something aloud because the au pair made a low *hmmph* in her throat. She said, "You used to come inside me so good. What's happened?" He tried to answer, but his tongue was thick and slow from the morphine.

Harriet, the au pair, peeled herself up from underneath him and stalked off in silence. On legs as lithe as an antelope's, she had run marathons right out of Africa until, at thirty-one, she couldn't run anymore. Her last race had been in Costa Rica, and once it was over, she stayed. With her pretty Kenyan English, she had posted an ad in the *Tico Times*, "Nanny for a wealthy expat." Dr. Parkinson had hired her right away.

Now the doctor lay naked on the bath mat, the question still looping in his ears. *Who am I and what am I doing?* But to this, he could come up with no answer. He lay there for a few more minutes before crawling out, into the master suite. Then he dressed, shuffled downstairs to the conservatory, and dropped into his vigil chair beside his wife Mary's hospital bed. Her breathing was shallow and vital signs faint. Her parents, with their hand-wringing and calling upon Jesus, paced in a nearby hotel in Escazú, waiting for a phone call, but he didn't call them. The maids were murmuring in Spanish and cooking something that smelled like curry in the kitchen; the kids were laughing and building a Lego castle in the living room, but he didn't interrupt.

He slumped in the chair and held Mary's hand, silent tears skidding down his stubbly jaw, until the house fell into shadows and sleep.

She died in the middle of the night, without waking up to say goodbye to him.

•

The funeral was attended by the regular circle of expats and Ticos that Sam and Mary had fallen into friendship with over the past five years. When asked how he was able to keep his head on straight, Sam reached over and squeezed Harriet's arm. "This woman right here," he said. "She's an angel disguised as an au pair." Harriet's lips protruded into a sheepish smile.

The Parkinsons didn't belong to a church, so Sam had Mary cremated and her ashes sealed in an urn, which he kept in the conservatory. In the days after the funeral, the maids surrounded the urn with Mary's favorite orchids just as they had done for her when she was drifting in and out of consciousness. While watering and dusting the plants, they often paused to stroke and kiss the urn. One of the little maids even propped a tiny image of the Virgin Mary against the handle.

A week had passed since Mary's remains rested in peace amongst her orchids, and every day Sam slithered home from the hospital, blasted the Jacuzzi full of hot water, and injected himself with enough morphine to kill a cat. Then he soaked, no jets, just the lovely vacuous water and steam and occasional screech of the parrots roosting in the high trees of the backyard.

One day the bathroom door creaked and vials rattled in the sink. Harriet's voice boomed in his ear. "You naughty naughty. What's this you're doing?" He slit his eyes open a crack, like a dog that doesn't want to be disturbed. She was wiggling an empty vial in his face.

He swatted the vial and her hand away. He said, "I'm lost. So?"

"So, I'm pregnant by you. Get out of that tub."

"What?" he said. The word boomed across the tile walls. "Can't be." He groaned and tried to lift himself out of the tub, but slipped and slid back on his wrists. Sputtering water, he held out one hand and begged, "Help me."

She towered over him, hands on hips. "Maybe I won't," she said. "Maybe I'll keep this baby and not give you any say about it." But then she stuck out one hand and hauled him up and over the edge so that he made a bumpy landing on the bath mat, his stocky bow-legs plastered with dark wet hair, his penis a pale grub. She threw a towel over his face. He patted dry, staring off at the beige bathroom walls so much like those at the hospital.

"Who am I?" he said, shaking his head. "Harriet?"

She was busy at the sink, scraping all the vials and needles into the trash can. She tied up the bag with a flourish, lifted it, and paraded out.

"No!" he cried. He pushed himself to his feet, but his body moved like a sluggish wet monster. It was like he was trying to run underwater in a swimming pool. By the time he reached the hallway, he heard the car door slam. He stumbled downstairs, towel falling off his middle, but she had already driven off with the precious potion he had come to crave in just a few short months.

•

That night, quaking headaches split Sam's skull as he muddled through homework sheets with his kids at the dining room table. Kristie and Jake both had received notes home. "At dismissal, Kristie repeatedly asks if her mom will be there today to pick her up." "Jake has trouble concentrating and steals crayons, lunch money, fluoride tablets, and other items from his desk buddies."

"Who am I?" Sam muttered, squinting and frowning over the notes.

Jake just said, "I don't know," and kept filling numbers in boxes next to different clusters of animals.

Kristie sat back on her heels and neatly replaced the cap on her pen. Lately she had discovered writing in ink. "Where's Mom?" she said. "She couldn't just disappear like that. Like *poof*."

"I wish I knew," Sam answered. He pretended to scan her long division.

"Do you think she's on another planet, maybe?"

"That's a distinct possibility," Sam said.

"I'd like to visit her just once." Kristie uncapped her pen again. She wrinkled her chin and added, "Maybe more than once."

Reaching over, Sam grabbed the Superman eraser from where it rested on the corner of Jake's worksheet. Howling, Jake stood up on his seat and shook. "Give it back," Jake yelled.

"No stealing," Sam said. "See how that feels? Stealing from others is like taking away from yourself. Then nobody feels good."

Jake stopped howling, but his hands remained in tiny balled fists. Sam set the eraser back in its place. Behind them, the night insects buzzed and chirped as loud as birds. He wondered where the pair of parrots went in the nighttime, if they just hung their heads and slept. He gazed at the stillness of the conservatory, the plants breathing their invisible breath around the ashes of his wife.

•

The next morning at the hospital, sweating and trembling, Sam journeyed up to the administrator's office. Briefcase in hand, he was piecing together an explanation for his haggardness— Mary's death, his kids' worrisome behavior at school. *Buenas vacaciones* the administrator said and thumped him on the shoulders. *Pura vida.* Probably Sam's appearance had done all the talking for him. He exited toward the elevators, but his head pounded so hard he wanted to bash his skull against the wall; his veins craved calm. He glanced back to look for the administrator before he ducked into the supply closet. He found the morphine and disposable needles and packed a dozen of each into his briefcase. What if he didn't come back for two weeks? He gathered six more vials. *Pura vida, my ass,* he thought.

•

Back home, he shot up in the bathroom and the wrecking ball in his head melted away. He was just easing himself into the water when Harriet flung open the door. She let out a great howl, rushed forward, and started slapping him. Kicking, he tried to push himself away, but the bottom of the tub was like a slip-n-slide and he inhaled water instead. He thrashed at her, but she came at him again, her slaps stinging his cheeks and neck like whips. Finally he struggled to his knees, grappled with her shoulders, and shoved her off. "This is who I am," he said.

She was wheezing and fighting to breathe. "What about the baby?" she asked.

"Too bad," he said.

"What are you going to do for me?" she said, sobbing into her palms. "You want to treat me like some piece of skin? I'll tell everyone the truth—how you disrespected Mary behind her back. And when she needed your love the most."

"I did love her. I'm one stupid prick without her. Don't you see?"

Harriet just cried louder and sank onto the rug. She balled up a towel and hugged it to her face. Sam stared, wanting the floating numbness of a few moments ago to return and this hysterical woman to shut up. He scooted up and out of the tub. At the sink, he prepared a small dose of morphine. Kneeling, he draped her arm across his lap. She sniffled and uttered a cry of protest. He said, "A little something to calm you down," and she reluctantly nodded, stifling a cry as the needle went in. A moment later, she was nestled on the rug, dozing, her legs splayed out in a somewhat obscene posture. He arranged the towel underneath her head as a pillow, tossed his robe over her, and hid the rest of the vials and needles in his shave kit. Then he hauled his limbs, heavy and sluggish with despair, downstairs for a glimpse of his kids.

The flat screen TV in the living room displayed a freeze-frame of video game instructions, the couches abandoned. He wandered through the dining room. A breeze washed over him, the back door of the conservatory open. The kids bent over something in the grass, talking in low, curious tones.

Slowly, he made his way to the doorway and slouched

against the frame. What had they found in the yard? "Kids," he called, but the single word was all he could manage.

Both of their shaggy, tangled heads shot up. Kristie jumped over to him, but Jake remained in his sturdy-legged squat over the patch of grass near the bushes.

"A lizard," Kristie said, out of breath. Strands of hair were caught in the corner of her lip. She grabbed Sam's loose arm and dragged him outside. "But it's not just a lizard. It's a sign from Mom."

Sam staggered over to the bushes where his kids were pointing, but saw nothing—just a mass of leaves and branches.

Jake clasped something in his tiny hands. "Look," he said, holding up the object. It was a round, decorated compact. Sam picked up the case, nearly fumbled the thing, but gripped hard and brought it up close to examine. The lid was orange leather studded with flowers and birds.

"It's the mirror Mom always carried in her purse," Kristie said. "We were going to play a video game, but then Jake saw this lizard sitting in the doorway."

"A big lizard," Jake said. He stuck his hands out to emphasize the size. "I almost got him but he ran away."

"We looked and we can't find him. But we found Mom's mirror in the bushes. Isn't that weird?" Kristie squinted up at Sam in the sunlight. "Dad? Are you okay?"

Sam still held the case flat in his palm. "I'm glad you found it." The compact had been one of his first gifts to Mary when they were dating, just after his divorce from his first wife. All Mary's things, he still had to sort through and get rid of them. He stepped back toward the house.

"Don't go," Kristie said. "It feels good to be outside, doesn't it?"

"You sleep too much," Jake said, and threw himself around

his father's leg. Sam eased onto one of the chaise lounges and promised he would watch for any big lizards. He rested the case on his chest. It had a tiny button at the bottom, and he kept springing open the lid and looking at himself in the small mirror, each time as if he might get an answer from his sunken reflection. But he didn't, so at last he clamped the case shut and watched his kids prance and romp. A pink and gold sunset filled the sky. When the maids called that dinner was ready, he was adrift on a raft underneath the rustling palms.

·

While Sam was holed up in his bedroom for nearly a week, Kristie wandered her school's open-air hallways with the bathroom pass and asked every janitor if they'd seen her mother. At one point, she locked herself in the girls' restroom and insisted she would only come out for Mary. Jake snatched juice boxes, cookies, and sandwiches from kids in the cafeteria. He stuffed what he could into his mouth and pockets, and hid the rest in his pant legs and waist. He pilfered his classroom, too—rulers, colored chalk, the bottle of pellets used to feed the class pet, Mr. Turtle, and even eye drops and mints were missing from his teacher's purse.

Emails and messages from the principal, teachers, guidance counselors, and gym coaches piled up. They demanded emergency meetings, which Sam tried to pawn off on Harriet. But she clucked her tongue and said, "You want me to be daddy and mummy both now? Sorry." He pleaded that he was too messed up to drive, and she relented.

Sam signed the kids out of school early that day, but had no idea what to say to them. Harriet took the driver's seat in the Galloper and didn't look at Sam once. The little unhappy family wound around the hills above Santa Ana in silence, the

Calle Vieja traffic stinky and balking. They turned onto their road. Some farmers were prodding three sets of trudging oxen up the hill, the yokes and carts brightly painted. A woman with young children on her lap rode in the back of one of the clattering carts. Kristie and Jake *oohed* and tapped the back windows.

Sam looked over at Harriet and said, "What would we do without you? You are like a gift from God."

Kristie and Jake were bouncing in their seats.

"Family takes care of one another," Harriet said.

·

The next day Sam reclined in the conservatory next to his wife's urn, hoping the proximity of Mary's remains would send some kind of shock wave through him, when Harriet tossed a Polaroid-looking photo onto his lap, a bean-like blob in the center. "Our baby," she said.

"Your baby," he said, sighing. "How much money do you want?"

"I'm not going anywhere," she said. "Why are you doing this?"

He didn't answer. Beneath the morphine, it was as if some great tide swelled within him and pushed him onward—a dangerous, swinging-from-the-chandelier type of feeling. Harriet disappeared upstairs and the skies above the glass ceiling churned grey and bellowed thunder. He fingered the top of the urn. There was no reason why this baby—a poor little life he didn't want, a burden—needed to be born. He fashioned an elaborate yet simple plan for a home abortion. He could perform the procedure by himself, in his master suite: sedate Harriet with morphine, rig up the IV stand left behind by Mary's hospice care with oxytocin and a blood thinner, pull up a chair and some towels and wait for the hemorrhage. It would be the middle of the night; Harriet would believe she had just miscarried.

Sam's plan brought him to the hospital, where he slipped into the obstetrics ward and found what he was looking for in a supply closet. That evening, sober as a saint, he powered through morphine withdrawal headaches and read up in his medical textbooks about the procedure. Across the hall, Jake was giggling as Harriet put him to bed. She sang to him in Swahili.

Sam stopped reading. He reached for the sonogram photo and was about to use it as a bookmark, but stared at the image and instead took a few long breaths. He touched the glossy photo—the pod was no bigger than his fingertip.

The wind gusting in the open windows cooled his face. From their scattered locales, neighborhood dogs exchanged barking conversation. The vast night made him think of Mary, no longer there—what if she was no more than a pod somewhere else now, starting over again? Without the morphine, every moment felt like being trapped inside a falling dream, but at the end of the falling there was an inevitable cracking open and the spilling out of who he really was—that pod of life still inside him.

Sam invited Harriet to bed that night.

·

A week later, Sam, Harriet, the kids, and the maids freed the house of Mary's things. Crates of Mary's clothes, her jewelry collection and hiking boots stacked up in the grass. Harriet suggested that the kids create a treasure box of items that belonged to their mother. Kristie decided she only wanted the orange compact found in the bushes, while Jake set about filling a shoebox with his mother's keychain, sunglasses, several of her favorite candies—Werther's Originals—and photos. Sam started to assemble his own Mary shoebox, then stopped. She was in everything and nothing. He carried the urn out into the driveway.

Kristie had tied one of her mother's old bikinis over her clothes and was spinning around the yard. She grabbed Harriet's hands and they danced with arms outstretched to the twittering of the insects and birds. "Do you know I can talk to my mom anytime and she's there?" Kristie said. "Do you know that, Dad?"

"We'll go out to Punta Leona," Sam said, "Or one of Mom's other favorite places with these ashes." He set the urn next to the back wheel of the Galloper and opened the trunk. "How about tomorrow?"

"You all go," Harriet said. "I'll stay here."

"Don't be silly," Sam told her.

Kristie dropped Harriet's hands and stamped her foot. "I'm *showing* you something," she said. "But you have to come out here." She waved Sam over.

Sam rumpled Kristie's hair, but she clapped her hand over his to make him still. He could feel the ever-so-slight rise and fall of Kristie's breath, how quiet she was being. He looked up at Harriet's closed eyes, her long neck and arms, as steady as the tree behind her with its orange petals, a wild color he had only seen before during the brilliant North American autumns of his boyhood. The cool air rushed over him; he stepped out of his flip flops to feel the warm earth underneath his feet and hopped at the shock of the burning hot grass. But he was remembering again.

Kristie took her hand off of his. "It takes practice," she said, and sighed dramatically. "But now you know." She skipped away and continued twirling around the yard.

Then Jake kicked his soccer ball across the quiet, and Sam turned his head just in time for the thud as the ball plowed into the urn and the ceramic broke on the macadam. The urn cleaved and fell in several pieces, spilling its contents into the lush green of the yard. Jake clenched his shirt, unmoving except for the whimpers of "I'm sorry" escaping his lips. Harriet glided over to him, clucking her tongue. "Now nobody's going to any pretty white beach," she chided.

They were moving ahead, Sam thought, although he marveled at how.

The pattern of Mary's bikini made a twirling blur in the distance until Kristie stopped. Sam watched as his daughter held out the orange compact like a compass and spoke to the mirror, "Now pay attention. Keep your mouth shut. Look around and listen."

Princess of Pop

The Princess of Pop remembered being a kid back in Louisiana on her cousins' wide wooden swing, climbing so high that with one release of the chain links she might sail off into the clouds. If only she could fly like the pretty quail her dad and uncles used to talk about when they returned from hunting, with the same look in their eyes as if they were talking about their latest girlfriend or a sexy movie star. But then they would unhitch the tailgate of someone's truck, toss aside the dirty canvas, and there would lay the quail, glossy soft feathers spotted with blood. "They fly fast but we get them eventually," her dad had said, lifting one by its feet and turning the bird so that she might see its beauty up close.

In her room at the Highland Gardens Hotel, the Princess of Pop traced her fingers along the smooth, empty dresser before swinging her oversized Fred Segal bag onto the bedspread. She yanked out the half-full bottle of Grey Goose, a container of blue-cheese-stuffed olives, a pack of Marlboro menthol lights, and two books: one given to her by Mel Gibson that was about Jesus saving the world from sin (she had managed to read a few chapters before losing interest); the other one, which she liked only slightly better, was called *A Confederacy of*

Dunces. Her older brother had insisted she read it because she liked to be funny, and he said she would appreciate the humor. And because she knew he was smart and she wanted him to think the same of her, she was struggling her way through the story so that the next time she visited him in New York they might have something to talk about besides their family sadness. But it had been months since she'd seen or spoken to her brother, and the corners of the book curled back, and the bookmark had disappeared last week. She shook out her little bottles of precious pills and they bounced and rolled across the comforter. She left them there, poured a glass of warm vodka, added two olives, then wandered to the balcony and leaned over the rail.

The Highland Gardens pool area was a secluded paradise. Palms bent over the walkways and birds twittered in the trees. No one was swimming; the pool gleamed a still, shining blue. But then someone shouted her name, and this startled her out of the quiet. That was her name, but she didn't know who that person was anymore; they might as well be calling someone else. Why did her life matter so much, anyway? But she followed the familiar throaty voices to the unshaven faces of the men ducking behind their cameras, lenses like the long black snouts of wild boar—her uncles used to hunt them, too, she remembered. *Click-click, click-click, click-click,* the cameras sounded like water guns. The men fired and waved from the balcony straight across from hers, on the opposite side of the pool.

She wanted to melt into her heels right there; she wanted to die. Instead she just held up her glass and said, "Cheers, boys." They were so busy shouting her name, though, the voices jamming atop one another, that she knew they didn't hear her. She peered down at the walkway below and listened, but no one was coming. Then she held the glass over the side of the balcony, let go, and waited for the splintering impact.

Nothing. When she leaned over the rail, she saw no broken glass anywhere. Where had the glass gone? It couldn't have just disappeared. Then she spotted it, nestled and whole in the long spiked leaves of a giant tropical plant underneath her balcony. The sunlight shone through and the glass had not a scratch; the two olives still floated on the bottom. She snorted, stalked back into the room and swayed with her arms crossed, not quite sure of what to do. The sheer white curtain liner puffed in the breeze. She poured herself another glass of vodka.

•

She decided to write a note to her kids. She found a Highland Gardens Hotel notepad and pen at the desk and began to write. But everything sounded false until she grabbed her cell phone and scrolled through to find a picture of her two sons. Only after staring into their dark eyes did the words she needed to say come out right. "Dear Boys," she wrote, "Mommy loves you but she can't be your Mommy anymore because she doesn't know how. She wanted love and a family so badly, but maybe she was just missing her own family too much. You will always be two wonderful bright shining stars, and Mommy knows that you will make her proud. But she has left for a good reason. You will be much better off without her around. Love and xoxos." She stared at the word, *Mommy*, another name that didn't fit, like a much-wished-for-but-too-snug gown that even the designer couldn't tailor to her size.

She found her iPod and cranked up the Janis Joplin song about the preacher's son. She had only discovered Joplin recently, much to her embarrassment. One of the nurses during her hospital stay had been humming one of the songs, and something about the melody sounded familiar, but she couldn't think of what. Her entire childhood had been spent singing along to show tunes for pageants, belting out Debbie Gibson lyrics for the Mickey Mouse Club, and later, blasting hip-hop as she practiced routines over and over with her dancers. Those songs had disappeared along with the past, but once she listened to *Janis Joplin's Greatest Hits* all the way through, something didn't let go. And then she found out the whole sad story one late night after staying up to watch *Hollywood Mysteries*. At least Janis hadn't left any children behind. Was it the music or the story of Joplin's life that so intrigued her? How did a woman her age, who had messed herself up with even more drugs and booze, end up creating music that stirred her soul? Her own albums had soared to Number One, had earned her the title Princess of Pop—but there was something missing in all those studio-conjured hits; they never made her shiver the way Joplin's songs did, even as she was recording them. This had so bothered her that three days before, at the screening of her latest music video, she fled the theatre after the first thirty seconds. She hated the woman onscreen because that wasn't really her; the electronic beats and the digitally altered voice weren't her own, either. None of it was real music. Her manager and agent ran after her, but by the time they caught up she was bawling so hard that she could barely talk. "All I ever wanted to do was dance," she said between chokes. "But they told me nobody ever got famous for just dancing." And the three of them stood there, the other two not saying anything.

She poured out the Xanax and Ambien and tapped the pills into two piles.

•

She stood naked in front of the bathroom mirror. Hot water blasted into the Jacuzzi and the steam rose like the offerings she'd seen people leave outside the Buddhist temple in L.A. She lifted handfuls of her hair and let it fall. But the person who stared back wasn't a girl anymore—she was a woman with a girl climbing out of her skin, and the face of the open-mouthed figure in the music video the other day belonged to someone else, a fabrication. Roots showed underneath her yellow hair. She remembered Bob, her first manager, the one who touched her while her mom was out running errands, saying to her mother, "Keep her as a blonde, just don't let the roots show. She's like a brand new Bardot." That was the summer right before her breakout hit. They were still living in Orlando, her mom and Bob, even though her dad and her brother and sister back in Louisiana didn't know that yet; her mom giggled and asked her all the time, "Can you keep a secret?" "Oh God, Mama," was her usual reply. But then the song hit the charts, the tour started, and they left Orlando.

For years, since becoming famous, the Princess of Pop dreamed about those early days in Orlando. She dreamed about going back and visiting a girl her age with long brown hair, just an ordinary girl she might have been friends with for the brief time she attended a normal high school, but she didn't know for sure if the girl was someone real or imaginary. When she saw the girl in her dreams, the scenario was always the same. She would show up at a club, and the girl would appear in the corner or next to her at the bar, and the Princess of Pop would grab the girl's hand, and they would run to the dance floor, laughing and dancing, just the two of them. But the girl never appeared on tour, or in a crowd of fans. Sometimes when the dream ended, the Princess of Pop woke up, her pillow damp with tears. Why did she keep dreaming about this girl she didn't even know existed?

She took a gulp of vodka straight from the bottle, stepped one foot in the tub. Another thing she still wondered: who is Brigitte Bardot?

•

The room phone rang and rang. In the hallway someone pounded at her door, called out her name. She had turned her phone off because the thing wouldn't stop lighting up, and besides, she had said her goodbyes. She eyed the hair dryer hanging from the wall. When she tried to steady herself in the scalding water, she teetered and clutched a towel bar for balance. That sure would be an easy way to die—a slip in the tub. No mess, no pain. But she leaned out, grabbed the dryer and flicked the switch; it roared to life. She pulled the dryer toward the tub to drop it in, but the curly cord yanked it back, so that the thing banged against the wall and swayed there, a blind, roaring head on a rope.

She crouched down in the tub, hugged her knees to her chest, and cried.

•

The sun was sinking, the sky darkening. She stood on the balcony again, wrapped in a towel, her hair drying in strings down her back, and shivered. In the pool below, a dark-haired young woman swam across the deep end like a frog.

She wished she could go down and talk to the woman— find out if she was from out of town, ask her if she had kids or divorced parents. Of course, the girl would recognize her. But what if she didn't? The thought sent a different chill. What if the girl was foreign, or had gone to Harvard? What if she didn't want to hear the Princess of Pop's side of things about the judge taking her sons away, or about buying millions of dollars in real estate for her parents? What if the girl asked her something like, "What's the most amazing thing you've ever done?"

The Princess of Pop would say, "Las Vegas." She wouldn't be able to look the girl in the eye.

"I'll bet you've never been to a museum," the girl might reply. And she would be right.

•

Janis Joplin was staying at the Highland Gardens when she died at twenty-seven, so perhaps it was no coincidence that the Princess of Pop had pointed her black Mercedes SUV in the hotel's direction when she peeled out of her Beverly Hills driveway that morning. All the way down the Sunset Strip, the photographers' vans trailed her. They dodged in and out of lanes like cats.

The Princess of Pop received the same treatment when she left the hotel in search of provisions, veering into the parking lot of the first pharmacy that appeared. Inside, the lights hurt her eyes. She bought scissors, more vodka, Rich Brown #27 hair dye, milk, and a box of Fruit Loops cereal. She stepped out, lit a cigarette, and blew smoke into the surrounding cameras. "What are you doing at the Highland Gardens?" the voices behind the cameras asked. "Where's the party?"

She pushed past them. "Why don't you throw one, if you're so interested?" she said. The photographers shoved into one another as they jogged to keep up with her, hurling questions like spears; their bodies pressed in so that she gasped for a breath of night air but instead choked on someone's cheap musk. She muttered, "How do you know I'm not here to pay my respects to Janis Joplin?"

"How long have you been a fan of Joplin?"

"Do you believe she killed herself?"

"What are you doing in a hotel room all alone? Everybody's worried about you."

She hauled herself into the SUV. "Maybe I'm going to kill myself," she said, shielding her eyes from the blinding flashes; she felt as if she was still wandering the illuminated aisles of the pharmacy. "Or maybe I just want to read a book," she said, and slammed the door.

•

Back in the hotel room, she read the instructions to the hair dye three times while singing along to Joplin's "Piece of My Heart." Soon she would transform into Rich Brown #27. She worked the chemicals into her scalp, draped a towel around her neck, and scooped the pills back into their bottles. Then she read a few pages of *A Confederacy of Dunces* and thought about Ignatius in his hunting cap. She didn't know anyone like Ignatius, only Hollywood people, but she guessed that his kind existed. Perhaps what she needed wasn't a disguise, but to actually *be* someone else.

She rinsed off the dye, combed out her hair, and read more of the book while her hair dried. Some parts made her laugh out loud. She couldn't remember ever laughing while reading the Jackie Collins novels her mother used to leave around the tour bus. But then she read the author's note in the back. The writer had committed suicide, and the book was published after his death, had even won prizes. She realized that even someone who created great work could feel as worthless as she did. How ridiculous she'd been to think that by reinventing herself—disappearing from Hollywood and starting her own dance academy for kids, for instance—those parts of her life that were most painful would change. Her father would still be aloof, her mother jealous, her ex a cheat, her younger sister an embarrassment, her brother loving but distant. I'll show them, she thought. I'll do it, and they'll have to think about how they ruined my life.

The phone rang, but she ignored it. She walked out on the balcony, eating the blue-cheese-stuffed olives, and the wind blew her hair across her face. She looked into the glowing water for the girl who had been swimming earlier, but the pool was as desolate as the moon. Only two photographers stood on the balcony across from hers. They were smoking; she could smell pot and cigarettes. They spoke in fast, private tones, and about sex; the breeze caught the words "pussy" and "tits" and carried them over. She remembered when the photographers first started following her everywhere. She had just turned sixteen and posed for the cover of *Rolling Stone*. One of them asked her if she'd had a boob job, and she lied.

She had changed her will the day before; now everything was in the names of her sons, still toddlers. They would have money for birthday parties, museums, college.

Now she waited for what seemed like a long time before the photographers noticed her, but neither of them picked up a camera. One of them slipped back inside. The other one lingered, clutching his beer bottle and looking up at the sky. Then across at her. He drained his beer, tossed the bottle into the bushes below, and called out to her through cupped hands. "We can still tell it's you," he said, just before disappearing inside.

She stood there in disbelief, her fingers rummaging through the last of the olives. She hurled one after another at their balcony. The olives struck the glass and scattered on the deck like BB pellets. "I hope you slip and fall, you assholes," she yelled. But no one opened the door even a crack.

The room phone rang again, and this time she answered it. The front desk clerk told her the hotel was concerned with the media vans and trucks crowding the parking lot and asked how long she planned to stay. "Why? Do I have to leave?" she asked. "You have my credit card, so swipe it."

"It's just that your presence is creating a disturbance for the other guests," the clerk said. "But of course, you may stay as long as you like."

"I'll be checking out shortly," she replied. Her voice was almost a whisper. She hung up. *Your presence is creating a disturbance.* She repeated that line to herself as she ate dry handfuls of Fruit Loops. Once again, she poured out the pills and divided them into two piles. *Your presence is creating a disturbance.* She grabbed the milk from the fridge, tore off the cap. After swallowing the first pile, she found her iPod and played "Summertime." She didn't know the words but hummed along as best she could. *Your presence is creating a disturbance. What else is there to do but create a disturbance?* She thought of Janis Joplin, who died in the very same hotel, perhaps down this very same hall. And the author who wrote about the funny guy wearing a hunter's cap on Bourbon Street, how did he perform his last dance? *I belong to a confederacy of dunces*, she thought and laughed because she didn't know what the title meant but saying it felt right. The last notes of "Summertime" faded away, and she downed the rest of the pills with the milk. *I belong to a confederacy of dunces.*

•

It wasn't long before she started throwing up. She crawled from the toilet to the phone by the bed and dialed zero. The clerk she'd spoken with earlier answered in the same crisp voice.

"Ready to check out, Princess?"

"I'm afraid I've created a disturbance," she said into the phone. "By killing myself. Please call my dad."

•

Someone rattled a key in the hotel door, and then she was surrounded by fast-talking, fast-moving men, but not paparazzi. These men were young and smooth-faced; they wore dark jumpsuits and lifted her onto a stretcher. The world opened out, and she was dashing along the brightly lit hallway as if swooping down a playground slide, everything on either side a blur. Voices babbled and called her name, but their tone was not like her brother coaxing her out to play when they were little. These voices wanted to know about the pills and the time, but her mouth wouldn't open to speak. In the lobby more voices rained down, high-pitched females joining the men, her chorus welcoming her back home.

"Is that the Princess of Pop, with the brown hair?"

"Did she finally kill herself?"

"Hang in there, gorgeous! We love you."

Outside she couldn't tell if it was night or morning; the light was as bright as day. She flew past a crowd holding up signs that said beautiful things: you are loved, Princess of Pop, you are a beautiful girl, you were born with creative genius. For the first time, she felt those things to be true. She tried to lift up one hand to wave, but her arm didn't move. She struggled to keep her eyes open and even though she was wrapped in blankets, she shuddered with chills. But she could still see enough to glimpse the faces of the crowd, to recognize her own image imprinted on t-shirts like the face of the Virgin Mary faded on a calendar she remembered in her grandparents' house. The person she had called for wasn't there.

One of the EMTs squeezed her hand; the others shouted for the throng to clear away from the ambulance doors. "Is my father here yet?" the Princess of Pop asked.

"He's on his way," the young man answered. He squeezed her hand harder and said, "Stay with me."

"Where is he?" she asked. "Is he hunting?"

"He's flying here as fast as he can, sweetie."

"I'm nobody's sweetie," she said.

"Okay then," he said and dropped her hand. They hoisted her into the back of the ambulance and shut the doors. The lights and noise vanished. She heard her own breathing, felt the jab of a needle in her arm, her blood draining away. The one who had clasped her hand before squeezed it again, leaned close, and said, "Stay, beautiful, stay."

The Sponge Diver

Nearly every day for six weeks, Melissa basked in pleasure at Jono's house. They savored imported cheese and beer by his pool. They kissed and tasted each other's salty mouths. They swam and laughed in the sunlit water, warm as a bath. But when Jono slid his hand to caress her below the waist, she entwined her fingers in his and pushed him away. There remained the problem of his deafness. Jono had lost seventy percent hearing in his left ear due to a sponge diving accident nineteen years earlier. Melissa had never given much thought to her expectations of a perfect man before—if such a person existed. She tried her best to squash any misgivings, and instead set her hopes on Jono.

"You're pressing too hard," Melissa said one afternoon. They were entwined on his bed, and she moved her hips as if she might succeed in bucking him off.

"Why won't you let me make you feel good?" He rolled away and perched on the edge of the mattress as if ready to bolt. "If you're not in love with me, just say so."

"I do love you," she said, scrambling to wrap her arms around him.

"Then what's wrong?"

"You're older," she said. "It's intimidating."

"Ever think how you might be intimidating?" he said. "Especially when you laugh and flirt like crazy one second, then shove me away the next?"

"I guess not. I'm sorry."

"I'm older, but I'm not crazy," Jono said. "You sure there's nothing else on your mind?"

"I'm fine," she said, toying with her necklace.

"I can tell if something's bothering you by your voice," he said. "The bum ear makes the other one a super listener."

She smiled and flung her arms around him, drawing him closer. "I want you to touch me," she said. "All over the place."

"What's that? Just remember which is my good ear." He reached across her thighs to tug open the nightstand drawer and fish out a condom—only to discover they had run out. "Figures," he said. "We could just pull out and pray."

"Are you kidding me?" she said. "What's so bad about wrapping it up, anyway?"

"You really don't know?" He shook his head in apparent disbelief. "Have you ever worn a wetsuit?" When she regarded him blankly, his eyes widened and his face slowly lit up. He ushered her off the bed and into the bathroom. "Get naked," he said.

"You don't have something kinky in mind, do you? I already told you, I'm not into that kind of thing—"

But he was in the hallway now, tearing through the closet. "Just you wait," he said, "this is going to be hilarious." A moment later he reappeared with a clear plastic poncho. Melissa warily stripped. "Put this on," Jono said, breathless with excitement. He cranked the shower on full blast and urged her to step in. After a solid minute of water beating down on the flimsy hood, she conceded that no, this wasn't the same as showering *au naturel* at all. She supposed they could investigate other options besides condoms, so she dressed and they headed for the closest pharmacy.

Each began at the opposite end of the display case and worked toward the center. Jono plucked a box off the shelf and examined the writing on all sides. "How about this?" he asked. "It's a sponge."

"I don't know," she replied. "I've never used anything like that before."

"Come on," he said, tossing the box in the air and catching it. "Where's your sense of adventure?"

"Sticking a plug up my cooch isn't exactly my idea of adventure."

"You just need to relax," he said. "The Hindu Cowboys are playing. We can go out, have a good time and then *bam*—we'll come home and slide that sponge in no problem."

This is trouble, she thought, staring at the sponge box and back to Jono, a shit-eating smile plastered across his face. The propaganda on the box read, "Ensures the steady flow of passion for a natural feel." So why did nothing feel natural about this?

"I think it's better if we stay in tonight," she said. "I don't want to stumble home and shove a sponge in wrong when I'm half-drunk."

Silently they sorted through the other boxes on the rack, but the other options, bullet-shaped gel inserts and an odd new condom from Japan, failed to convince her.

"No big deal," Jono said wearily, grabbing a new Trojan tri-pack.

As they proceeded toward the checkout, a display near the

school supply section caught her attention. A deluxe edition of Scrabble. She ran a finger along the box.

"Let's make a deal," Jono said. "I promise we can make dinner at home and play Scrabble afterwards, if you'll at least come out with me for a couple hours." When she didn't answer, he said, "You know, being in a relationship is a two-way street. I can't be with someone who's not willing to meet me on the most basic level."

"Okay, it's a deal." As soon as she said it she felt dishonest, like the deal she was making was really against herself.

"And we try the sponge," he said. "Tonight. Just once."

She grimaced when she pictured the sponge package. The crude insertion instructions reminded her of drains, or sealing up a manhole.

"Maybe it won't be so bad. Like my hearing aid." He tilted his deaf ear toward her as he spoke. "I got used to wearing it."

She told him to get it.

He hurried back to the family planning aisle. Just as he was about to turn the corner, she said, "Hold on." She thought she said it pretty loudly, but Jono disappeared past the two-for-one tampon display.

•

That night Jono made good on his promise. Over grilled lamb kebobs and then the Scrabble game, he told more stories about his family and his many Greek relatives who still lived in Tarpon Springs. Hardly any of his generation had stuck around to preserve the sponge diving tradition. Melissa begged him to play one more game, this time using only foreign words so she could practice her French, but he packed up the game and blew out the candle. Already it was nine-thirty. The earlier they went to the show, the sooner they could be back.

Galloping banjos pounded from the small stage as Jono led Melissa toward the bar. "Great, huh?" he shouted into her face.

She only ventured out to clubs for blues or jazz, and at home sometimes put on old cabaret, but she nodded. Jono asked her what she'd like to drink. She told him a rum-and-Coke. His face scrunched into a mixture of surprise and dismay, but he held up his finger to indicate he'd be right back.

About ten minutes passed and Melissa wondered where he had gone. To her surprise, she was really into the music, and so wanted to find out more from him about the band. Then she saw him walking toward her. He held out a box of Marlboros.

"This is all they had," he said. "Hope that's okay."

"What?" She shook her head.

"Thought you said you wanted to smoke."

She shook her head again. "Rum-and-Coke," she said.

"Oh," he said. "Sorry. It's pretty impossible for me to carry on a conversation when I go out in a noisy place like this."

"I'll get the drink," she said.

But Jono flagged the bartender down.

When Melissa finally sipped her cocktail, she noticed it tasted strange. She took another sip before realizing that Jono had ordered her a rum-and-Diet Coke. Tapping his shoulder failed to grab his attention though, so she hung back. He bobbed and rocked to the tunes. Between the bodies packing in, the smoke, and Jono's towering frame, she couldn't even get a decent view of the band. In an effort to show patience, she forced down a quarter of her drink—she loathed diet—before she got across that she wanted to go. Now.

On the ride home Jono rattled off nonstop about the Hindu Cowboys. Melissa remained silent. Why couldn't she get over a simple handicap and accept that Jono was a little different?

He even encouraged her obsession with demystifying French culture, a fascination which previous boyfriends had either deemed too perplexing, tried to ignore, or both. With these past dating partners and lovers, she had more often than not begged, even bribed, to see a French movie at the local art house cinema, or dine at one of the few French restaurants in town, Chez Vincent (the reluctant partner would undoubtedly pronounce "chez" like "fez"). But Jono enjoyed foreign films in general and spoke enough French to use *liaisons* in ordering off a menu.

Back at his house, she trailed behind Jono's lumbering, fast pace, and once inside he pressed close and kissed her.

The sponge resembled a miniature inflatable raft, but for all its strangeness, it posed no problems that night. They joked about it, which lightened the mood. Still, Melissa grew anxious about leaving such an odd-looking, man-made object inside her for too long. She reached for the box on the bedside table. The directions said she could remove it six hours after having sex, but suddenly she couldn't wait to get the thing out of her.

In the bathroom, she ran into one problem after another in her attempts to persuade the sponge out. First she couldn't find the string. She tried to hook the edge of the device with her finger; the sponge turned like a globe on its axis but refused to move downward. After varying attempts of squatting, breathing, squeezing different muscle groups and rereading the microscopic instructions, she burst out of the bathroom and shook Jono awake. "You have to help me," she said, and explained to him in detail the situation.

He rolled over and hugged the pillow. "Nope," he said, voice muffled. "I'm not pulling that thing out."

"But the only reason I'm in this position is because of you!"

"You just need to relax more. Why do you want to take it out now anyway?" He lifted his head and spoke with a grin. "Maybe I want to have sex again."

"You've got to be kidding me," she said.

"You'll get it out," he replied. "Come back to bed, will you?"

Melissa ducked into the bathroom and sat naked on the toilet. Why did he act like he wasn't concerned in the least? She poked the sealed sponges remaining in the box and thought his refusal funny and irritating, the irony that Jono had once gone sponge diving and lost his hearing, but was now unwilling to help her retrieve a different type of sponge. What kind of guy treated his new girlfriend like that, especially a smart, attractive, twenty-years-*younger* girlfriend he should consider himself lucky to catch? A dick, that's what kind.

She remained there for a few minutes, her head on her palm like the Rodin sculpture featured in her French grammar book. So what if Jono wasn't the real problem—maybe the problem was her. Hadn't she always savored Degas' ballerinas and skipped over Picasso's blue period because she preferred ease to noise?

•

She arrived home that night only to spend another two hours bending, probing, and cursing the sponge, wedged tight as a cork. Since it was the weekend, she would have to wait until Monday morning to call her doctor and make an appointment. She called Jono every hour to report her lack of progress, but he didn't answer, and she wondered if he wasn't picking up on purpose or if he didn't hear the phone. In the middle of the night, after spending several hours reading articles online about Toxic Shock Syndrome, she considered driving herself to the ER, but figured she still had some time. Shortly before dawn she fell into a restless sleep.

Midmorning, the buzz of her phone jerked her awake. "Guess you didn't hear your phone last night," she said.

"Why wouldn't I hear it?" he replied, an edge to his tone.

"Because I called," she said slowly, "about a million times. Why didn't you pick up?"

"So, I'm calling you now, aren't I? How about some brunch?"

All the pent-up frustration of the night before morphed into fury. How could he be so insensitive, to send her home with a sponge stuck inside her and not even think to call? Did he think human beings could just amble about willy-nilly with foreign objects lodged in body cavities? Had he thought for a minute what her night had been like—fretting over whether her fears warranted a hefty ER bill, and worse, that he could care less.

On the other end Jono remained silent. He was sorry, he said, but he'd gone out to the Copper Rocket pub to catch another band and hadn't checked his phone until now. He pleaded for her to come over, and he would try his best to help her. "I was just having some fun with you," he said. "I didn't realize you were so freaked out, honestly."

"I'm not going anywhere," she flatly replied. "Unless it's to a clinic that's open on weekends."

He snickered. "Will you quit it with the paranoia already?"

"I'm giving you until noon to get over here," she said. "Then I'm going and sending you the doctor's bill. This was all your idea."

At ten minutes to twelve, she was about to grab her keys and go when Jono showed up at her front door. He hugged her and apologized repeatedly. He then gave her a present of designer jeans, a silk blouse, and a miniature stuffed sheep made from real wool, which made her laugh. "That's to get you to relax before the procedure," he said with an airy confidence. "I figured out how to do this."

And the sponge popped out.

•

The following Saturday, Melissa and Jono once again lounged poolside. They sat at opposite sides of his patio, each pecking at a laptop. With her trip to France approaching, Melissa was listening to a program that crooned out simple French phrases, a pronunciation exercise which recorded and rated her replies. Jono jumped up and paced. "Let's go to a show or something," he said. "Maybe I should make a few phone calls, find out what bands are playing."

"A band, like what we did last week?" she said. "Isn't that bad for your hearing?"

He didn't answer. She shouted a few times and finally had to grab his arm to get his attention.

"I'll just wear my hearing aid," he said. "I thought you said you like concerts."

"I do," she said, squelching the image of them arm-in-arm in a packed bar, his hearing aid sticking out for the world to see. She repeated the phrases the bewitching female voice emitted from the laptop, "Where is the cat? *Ou est le chat?*"

"Or a play," he suggested. "*To Kill a Mockingbird* is playing. Eight o'clock."

"The cat is on the table," the laptop said.

Melissa frowned. "Could we maybe squeeze in a Scrabble game?" To the recording she answered, "*Le chat est sur le table.*"

"If you'd rather stay in, that's fine. But I hope you're better at French than this, right?" He sank into the seat nearby and dragged her onto his lap, closing her laptop with his other

113

hand. Mid-sentence, the lilting French interrogation cut off.

"I'm just brushing up," she said quickly. He kissed her neck, but she pulled back. "I like going out," she said. "Only I like staying home even more. Isn't this nice?"

"Are you afraid of me or something?" he asked. "Sometimes you act—repulsed."

She let out a nervous laugh. "I don't know what you're talking about."

He shoved her off. "You sure? Look at me."

She scooted back onto the chaise lounge and grappled with her laptop, opening its face. "No, I'm not going to." When he reached for her chin to jerk it towards him, she shrank back. "This is stupid, you can't make me"—and he abruptly got up.

"I want you to leave," he said. "Right now. And don't bother to call or stop by." He roamed the patio with his unwieldy walk for a few minutes, his breaths labored and jerky.

She tried to respond, but her thoughts were jumbled. A vague whimpering protest was all that escaped her lips.

"You think I'm kidding?" he said. He was pitching her things into her pool bag, speaking in a rasping voice that scared her. "Your little act, I've got it all figured out. Even if you don't. Now get the hell out."

He trailed her as she gathered the rest of her things and sullenly climbed into her car. She sat there for a minute, vents on full blast, waiting for the air to cool down as she knew it would. When she looked again, he'd gone inside. She spotted him in the dim kitchen, shirtless. He had balled up his t-shirt and with his back to her, rested against the counter. Then he picked up his hearing aid, jammed it into his ear and disappeared from view. *Well then*, she thought, *it's done*. She plugged in her iPod. An Edith Piaf song burst to life, the lamenting wail reverberating throughout the baking vehicle. Too shocked and ashamed to sob or curse, she backed down the drive. In the trapped heat she was unaware of anything but the singer's crackling, yearning voice.

Don't Forget the Beignets

Merly froze in the doorway of her New Orleans hotel room where three FBI agents had her fiancé, Alan, seated and handcuffed. "What the hell is going on?" she asked. Alan just gawked at her and said, "I'm sorry," over and over again. Quivering, she looked from one agent to another for an explanation, then charged for the chair. One of the agents blocked her path, but she pushed her way through. She gripped Alan's arm with both hands. "But our life," she said.

Alan stared back with a look reminiscent of a cow who knows the truck is bound for the slaughterhouse.

She said, "Everything's ruined. Everything's gone. Why?"

"Conspiracy to commit securities fraud, for one," the agent beside Alan answered. He and the other two chuckled in their throats. The smart-mouthed agent said, "You can take possession of his personal belongings, but then you're responsible for whatever evidence might be in them. I would lock them up with the hotel manager if I were you, until he makes bail."

"Great," she said, blinking back tears. As if on cue, the lead agent handed her a Kleenex from atop the dresser. He scrawled something in his notepad, ripped off the paper and handed it to her. She dropped her chin and folded the sheet without reading it.

They hauled Alan to his feet and jerked him out into the hall, handling him as if he might spring away like a wildcat when he moved more like a lumbering bear. Merly trotted after them, wobbly-kneed and stammering. "What do I do now?" she asked.

"Everything's going to be fine," Alan called over his shoulder, "I love you, honey." But she couldn't answer; it was as if her words were stuck in the brick walls and ornate brass furnishings. She stared at Alan's wad of hundred dollar bills and rose-colored *colones* bound together by a plastic binder clip, the suitcase with his favorite tie-dyed sarong draped next to her perfect black cardigan, and his athlete's foot cream, uncapped and abandoned on the nightstand. In the air-conditioned coolness, she felt as if someone or something had just died. But was that so? Outside, a horse-and-carriage clopped past.

She read the agent's note, which provided numbers for the Orleans Parish Prison. FEDERAL POD the agent had noted, with double underlining. How could Alan have behaved so irresponsibly that he would do this to her? She had questioned him time and again about his business of off-shore banking and investing, and he insisted that they had nothing to worry about. She was young, after all, only twenty-four at the time, just a copywriter for his investment firm in Costa Rica. Had he been lying all along? What else had he been keeping from her? She pictured Alan in a jumpsuit and the agents questioning him in a grey, bare room, like in the movies. Was it possible that he had been unknowingly roped into a bad deal by a disgruntled client who wanted to bring him down? She grabbed her sweater, shoved the telephone number in her purse, and left.

•

Merly had only been to New Orleans once before, with Alan. He'd been a longtime fan of the French Quarter and often talked about moving there once his kids finished high school. She and Alan were supposed to be tagging along with real estate agents, roaming the Marigny Triangle for rentals, munching beignets and sipping coffee at Café du Monde. But now she walked at a clip, alone.

It was shortly after eleven a.m. and the streets were jammed with parked cars, four-way blinkers flashing. Half of the restaurants and shops stood dark. The Quarter reeked of hot asphalt and clogged gutters. A hurricane had blown to the west three days before, and the city evacuated. Now residents flooded back, dragging suitcases up to their wrought-iron balconies. No street musicians scratched at their harmonicas, no fiery geraniums brightened the windowsills, no sneaker-clad tourists bounced around but for her.

At Jackson Square, she decided to cut through and study the statue of the seventh president on his horse. Once she had written a fine history paper on Andrew Jackson, and now she recalled striking similarities between him and Alan. Jackson had fought against private banks like the Federal Reserve, while Alan evaded the IRS. He claimed the monetary system was built on illegal fiat currency, and such a system made slaves of taxpayers. But now Jackson was dead and long forgotten except for the twenty dollar bill, and Alan was in jail. She could do nothing to change that.

What was she still doing in New Orleans? She should fly

back to Sarasota, start packing up her things. They weren't married; Alan's Florida home wasn't in her name. She could just leave. But then she thought of the other house in Costa Rica—the six-month-old street dog they had recently adopted, her books and closet of clothes. She couldn't just leave all that behind, could she? Part of her was secretly glad. She hated living in Costa Rica, even part-time. She hated the litter blowing in the street gutters and underneath the eucalyptus trees of Sebana Park, the way she had to remember to remove her watch and earrings before visiting the downtown market, the drivers who made their own lanes in the median to bypass traffic. And if she flew there alone to pack up and fire the maids, she would have to face all the rattled employees, explain to their neighbors and expat friends. Why should she have to clean up Alan's mess?

·

In the lobby, the hotel manager regarded Merly with a knowing yet empathetic smile. But as she approached the desk to discuss an early check-out, the manager spoke first. "Ma'am, someone is waiting for you," he said in his lilting drawl. "Your cousin?"

She followed his finger to the hotel restaurant. Her cousin Carol sat at a table set for three, her large chest squeezed against the pressed white tablecloth. Carol sported the same short, professionally cut-and-colored coif that she'd maintained for the last twenty-five years. She arose slowly to greet Merly, arms outstretched.

Merly had entirely forgotten that they had arranged to have lunch with Carol.

"Where's your beau?" Carol asked, glancing over Merly's shoulder as if Alan was a new dessert she had been looking forward to trying. She wore earrings made out of Mardi Gras beads: purple and green and gold. When Merly replied, "In jail," Carol burst into laughter; her earrings shimmied.

"It's serious," Merly told her.

Carol's face flushed from joy to a delighted shock that indicated a lifetime of soap-opera watching. "No!" she gushed, and clutched Merly's thin shoulder with her plump, manicured hand. "Sweetie, what happened?"

Merly described the scene of Alan's arrest.

Carol said, "Well, I guess that ends that. You can't have a fiancé who's in jail. How many years have you been with this sugar-daddy?"

"I've got my own mind," Merly replied. "And I love Alan. I'm just not used to the FBI ending my relationships for me."

The waiter showed up and asked if they would be dining. Merly told him no and Carol told him yes simultaneously. Carol ordered a shrimp po'boy and said the occasion called for a Pimm's Cup. Merly ordered an herbal tea. The waiter, a frail-looking, white-haired man whose brass nameplate proclaimed him to be DORIS, raised his eyebrows as if ordering a hot herbal tea was the worst faux pas one could commit when visiting New Orleans. When he returned with the beverages, his gloved hand shook so that Merly's teacup jostled in its saucer. "You've got to think about *you*," Carol was saying. "Are you working?"

"I've been writing my book on gastric bypass surgery. Alan's been supporting me entirely."

"You could still move here." Carol sucked down her cocktail by an inch. "Stay with me until you finish your book."

Merly mopped up the spilled tea in her saucer and avoided meeting her cousin's gaze. Carol had never married but had a history of enough deadbeat boyfriends to fill a federal pod. Besides, Merly didn't know much else about her cousin, other than that she sold liability insurance.

"Thanks for the offer," Merly said. "But I've got to talk to him one-on-one first. I've got to find out why he allowed himself to get in this much trouble. It just doesn't make sense." She shook her head. "Alan loves his kids. He would never knowingly risk our whole future just to make money."

"But that's what you're not understanding, sweetie," Carol said. "Of course, he would never *knowingly* cross the line if he thought your lives would be ruined, but that's the way the criminal mind operates. He thought he was going to get away with it. Trust me, sweetie, I know. This is New Orleans." She swept her palm overhead, her booming voice sounding almost like pride.

Merly said nothing. Carol asked her about the gastric bypass book because she'd been thinking about undergoing the surgery. Merly sketched out an overview of *Why You Should Go Offshore for Gastric Bypass Surgery*, but she was too distracted to elaborate beyond that. She told Carol she wanted to check out early, even though the room was paid for two more nights and it was a waste to change the plane ticket. She balled up her cloth napkin and threw it on the table.

"You go down and get yourself some beignets at Café du Monde," Carol said. She signaled for the check to Doris the waiter, who was polishing silverware in the corner of the dining room and nodding off. "Keep asking yourself if you're up for this courtroom drama to play out. You're not even thirty yet. What about what *you* want?"

The bill arrived and Merly pulled out a twenty from the stack in her Fendi wallet; Alan had supplied her with several hundred dollars upon their arrival in case she needed cash in an emergency. Until that morning, she had always equated "emergency" with scenarios of him dropping from a massive heart attack and her stepping out of the shower to find the body. She had harped on him for years to take walks after work, cut out cigars, shop organic, and the whole time the FBI had Alan red-flagged, monitoring his emails and tracking bank wires. What a fool I am, she thought.

"My treat," Carol said, and reached for her wallet. "You aren't going to keep seeing him, are you? If he was taking advantage of other people, I guaran-goddamn-tee he was doing the same to you, sweetie."

Merly slid over the silver tray with Andrew Jackson. Hot tears blurred her vision. "You know what? I will stay the weekend. Why should I let this ruin everything?" She jumped up from her chair and didn't bother to push it in, but when she whipped around with her purse she ran straight into Doris, nearly knocking him to the floor. She apologized, extended a hand to steady him, and fled.

•

Two hours later, Merly was making her way through a second plate of beignets while working on a chapter of her book at Café du Monde. It was the section recounting Alan and his life-long battle with weight, how he finally arrived at the decision to undergo gastric bypass surgery in Costa Rica, where the doctors were graduates of top American med schools but offered the same procedure at less than half the price. She was stuck on the follow-up paragraph to Alan's quote: "I finally looked in the mirror one day and admitted to myself that I was an out-of-control extremist. I could have turned into a money pig or a sex pig, but instead I literally blew up into a giant pig." Her pencil hovered and wrote, scratched out, wrote again, scribbled over. Alan no longer tipped the scales at three hundred pounds, but was he now merely a grubby-handed pig in a slimmed-down body?

Powdered sugar carpeted her black sweater. The same thing had happened when she and Alan ate here last year, only they had come at night for dessert. She wore a black dress, Alan a dress shirt and Jerry Garcia tie. No beignets for Alan this time, just the Orleans Parish Prison food, which he probably deserved for gambling their future away. He'd probably forgotten all about how these beignets were his favorite things in the whole world, but she hadn't. Maybe she'd pay a visit to him while she was still in town, show him how much she was enjoying herself. After all, this might be her only opportunity. The Feds might not allow him bail if they believed him to be a high flight risk. She wrapped the remaining beignets in several layers of napkins and tucked them in her purse, then paid and stepped into the afternoon, sunny with a warm breeze. From the waterfront, the calliope on the deck of the half-empty paddleboat blasted into song. Knowing that she wasn't going to jail shed a strange, startling light on everything, so that even to walk around and eat beignets and watch the passersby was no longer a small thing, but rather the heartbeat of life itself.

•

Back in the hotel room, the maids had tidied up the bed and sink, but otherwise the room appeared like any other couple's romantic vacation quarters: the dress shirts hanging in the closet, the video camera charging in the socket, the shave kit opened, fuzzy pink handcuffs in the zipper pocket. Merly had set her phone on silent, and a dozen voicemails awaited— from Alan's mother, his kids, his lawyer, his rabbi, and several employees at his Costa Rica office. The last message was from Alan. He repeatedly apologized and rendered assurances of love. In a quiet but clear voice, he asked if she would visit tomorrow between two and four if she was still in the city. At the end he broke down, mumbled something about all the pressure he'd been under from his debts, confessed that he didn't deserve her, and hung up.

Merly returned none of the messages. Instead she worked on the manuscript until the sun sank into the Mississippi and the night stretched out empty before her.

•

The next morning, Merly dressed in a skirt, high-heeled sandals, and make-up. She returned the previous day's calls and gave out Alan's mother's number as his contact person. She phoned each of his kids: the two sons were monosyllabic at best; she and Alan's daughter, only nineteen, lamented together. A longtime expat friend phoned with an update. "This is big, Merly," he said. A.M. Costa Rica had just sent out a newswire that the FBI and equivalent Costa Rican agency had raided Alan's San José office on Paseo Colon that morning, hauling out computers and filing cabinets in front of dozens of stunned employees. Merly could see each one of their faces: the young Ticas who relied on their secretarial jobs so they could attend university at night, the fledgling stockbrokers who had looked up to Alan like a father.

She stopped by Café du Monde for a hot bag of beignets right before hailing a cab and heading to the prison. The scene played over and over in her mind—Alan would no doubt beg his innocence, plead with her to stick by him, and rattle off a to-do list for her. That was when she would stand up and take the beignets out of her purse and wave them in front of the glass. Perhaps he would even be able to smell the beignets and think of the memories he had taken for granted. And she would take out a beignet and bite into it right there, just to be mean.

But when she arrived, the guard made her check her purse into a locker before they allowed her in the visiting area. How stupid, she thought. Of course, bringing in the beignets was impossible. Now what could she do? She might brag about her afternoon of writing and enjoying beignets yesterday, but that didn't carry quite the same effect. She would think of something.

A guard led her to a plastic chair in front of the glass window and, a moment later, Alan appeared on the other side. He wore a baby blue sweatsuit and looked like a giant toddler. The thinning hair around his bald spot stuck up every-which-way. He smiled a weak smile when he saw her. The hulking guard who escorted Alan unshackled his wrists and ankles, then left. Alan and Merly sat across from one another and picked up the telephones, but she waited for him to say something first.

"Are you okay?" he asked. "Did you meet up with your cousin?"

She was shocked that he remembered this, but nodded. "It was a disaster," she said, then told him how she had to explain everything to Carol. "I got so upset, I knocked over the waiter."

"I'm sorry," he said. "It's all my fault."

"No more apologies," she said abruptly. "Please be straight with me about this. The FBI just doesn't pick up people for nothing." She thought of telling him about the raid in Costa Rica but thought better of it.

He lifted his chin and looked at her steadily. "It was a set-up," he said. "One of the brokers we've been dealing with recently was an undercover agent, and we offered him a kickback. It was a stupid thing to do." He leaned in close and pressed his nose against the glass. "I love you," he said, voice shaky. "I was so worried that you wouldn't show up today, that you had gone back to Florida."

"So all the times I've asked you about the stock deals, you haven't been lying?"

His face crumpled on the other end. "Never," he said, his tone indignant. "Look, the stock market is like Vegas. Only in Vegas if you gamble and lose, you can't file a complaint against the casino. On Wall Street, you can. Someone we did business with filed a complaint, and then the FBI set up this investigation. They reeled me in unknowingly. A sting."

"The whole thing sounds corrupt to me," she said. "How do you know who to trust?"

"You don't," he said, shrugging. "But have I ever lied to you about anything else?"

Merly thought over their three years together. She only remembered the good times—how she had brought an ice cream maker down to Costa Rica one time for Alan to make homemade ice cream for his kids. Last year he had even paid for all of his employees, including the maids who emptied the office trash, to go to Cancún for the weekend—and booked the entire first class compartment of the airplane for the hourly wage staff while he and Merly sat back in coach. She couldn't recall any time that she suspected Alan of hiding something from her other than a birthday surprise. "I forgive you, no matter what you did," she said. "And I'll always be your friend."

"I wanted us to get married here this weekend," he said. He held the phone with one hand and covered his eyes loosely with the other. "I want to be with you for the rest of my life."

"Well, that's not going to happen now," she replied. "How is it in there?"

He cracked a smile. "You wouldn't believe this place. Guys shooting heroin, smoking weed, cell phones going off."

"I ate a whole plate of beignets yesterday," she said. "At Café du Monde."

"You did?" His eyes filled with tears. "I'm glad."

Alan planted his face into the sleeve of his sweatshirt, where the word FEDERAL ran down the side, and bawled. His sobs echoed on the other side of the glass; on her end, the guards talked and joked. She tapped the glass, and Alan lifted his head, receiver limp in his hand. "I want to die," he moaned.

She told him that he couldn't act like a lump; he had to pick himself up and post the bail the Feds wanted—over a million dollars. He needed to hire the best lawyers on Wall Street. But she only had one more day left, and then she was going back to Sarasota to finish her book. He begged her to stay; in a few days, when he posted bail, they could still walk through Jackson Square and sip coffee at Café du Monde. But she couldn't promise that, she said.

"Why not?" he asked, seeming genuinely shocked.

"Because I've got to live my own life. I don't want to be the mafia widow in the courtroom, watching you get dragged off to spend the next twenty years in jail."

They exchanged a long, sober look. Alan's chin quivered. At last he said, "If only I'd followed my passion for cooking, none of this would have happened."

They both hung up their phones. Alan kept staring at her as she stood up. She gave him a little smile and a wave, felt his eyes boring into her back. As soon as she stepped into the hall, she started crying and wiping her face.

The guard said, "Ma'am, can I get you some Kleenex or something?"

She nodded vigorously, managed to ask for her purse. A moment later, he delivered it and she fumbled around for the mini-pack of tissues she always carried. The purse was stuffed with beignets, still warm in their waxed paper bag. Finally she found the tissues.

"Mmm, that sure smells good," the guard said. He stood with his arms folded but craned his neck toward the handbag. He looked like he subsisted on nothing but protein shakes.

She dabbed her eyes and collected herself. "Fresh beignets," she said slowly. "Best in town. From Café du Monde."

"Oh, yeah?"

She held out the bag. "Why don't you take a couple for yourself? And make sure the big guy who's sitting back there behind the glass gets the rest."

"I don't know about that, ma'am."

The blood throbbed in her neck and chest, but she dug once more in her purse, this time for the secret spot where she hid cash in case her wallet was stolen. She withdrew the neatly folded twenty, Andrew Jackson's stark face looming, tucked the bill underneath the bag and offered it again. "Best beignets in town," she said tauntingly.

The guard watched her do this and grinned. "I sure do appreciate your kindness," he said.

"I'll just wait here a minute and clean myself up while you go attend to my fiancé." She was still holding out the bag. "He's sure looking sad behind that glass."

At last the guard snatched the bundle, crammed a beignet in his mouth, and strolled off. Seconds later, he reappeared on the other side, munching the greasy dough ball with one hand and tapping Alan on the shoulder with the other. The guard said something and Alan got up. The guard cuffed Alan, who managed to give Merly an I-love-you in sign language as they rounded the corner, out of sight.

Only then did she realize she had no way to tell if the guard would carry through on giving Alan the beignets or not. There was nothing for her to do but zip her purse shut and head out. New Orleans might be the most corrupt city in America, but perhaps such corruption ushered in more compassion, and that allowance for human errors meant allowance for greater forgiveness, too.

•

Three days later, Alan posted bail. Merly brought his passport so he could forfeit it. She co-signed the bond, a part-cash and part-assets deal. Alan put up his million-dollar house in Sarasota. In exchange, the Feds granted him restricted travel to Florida, Manhattan, where Alan would be tried, and New Orleans, since that was where he "got pinched," as he put it. He was required to call a number once a day and check in.

They didn't say much on the ride to the hotel. The cab passed by sidewalk cafés bustling with lunchtime patrons; the smells of Cajun spices and seafood drifted in the half-opened windows. As they neared Jackson Square, she glanced over at Alan. He gazed out, as if looking for something he'd lost. She placed her hand on his and he jumped.

"Sorry," she said.

"I want to walk around," he said. "Forget everything for awhile."

They stopped by the hotel for Alan to shower and change out of his wrinkled clothes. Merly called Carol to give her an update and invited her to join them for coffee. Carol admitted her surprise that Merly was still in town and with Alan, but she said she wouldn't miss meeting him for the world, not after she'd heard so many colorful things about him.

The three met at Café du Monde. Alan bought cigars and insisted they smoke them to celebrate his release. Merly gagged on hers but Carol lit up like a pro, leaned back, and rested one pudgy foot on the opposite chair. Alan tossed his binder clip of cash onto the table, and Carol exclaimed, "A binder clip for a wallet?" She nudged Merly. "Where'd you meet this guy?"

"A rich man who's honest always carries his money inconspicuously," Alan said. He held up the cash and added, "It's the Wall Street types with the silver Tiffany's clips you gotta watch out for."

Carol laughed. They ordered one plate of beignets and then another. By late afternoon, Carol had locked in a date for gastric bypass surgery and booked a plane ticket to Costa Rica. She offered up her house on Frenchman's Street for when she'd be gone. "You can finish your book there," she suggested. Alan and Merly looked at one another. "Maybe," Merly said.

After Carol left, they stayed in the café past sundown. Merly took out a notepad and started making lists. Alan's overseas bank accounts would likely be frozen. They would have to sell his watches, his paintings in Sarasota; perhaps they could sell the cars in Costa Rica to neighbors for a fair price. A Wall Street lawyer would cost hundreds of thousands of dollars. She adjusted her bracelet, an early gift from Alan. "I'll sell my jewelry," she said.

Alan stared at his toes. "You keep that," he said. Then he leaned over, his breath warm and bitter from the cigars, and slid his arm across her shoulders. "Kiss me," he said.

Her heart raced in a way that made her stomach clench. She inched away and quietly said, "I can't." His arm dropped back, and he crushed the end of his cigar in the ash tray.

On the sidewalk outside the café, a man rolled up with a huge telescope. He climbed a short stepladder and adjusted the angle at which the telescope was pointed at the sky, then propped a cardboard sign at the base: ONLY $15 FOR 15 MINUTES WITH THE STARS! REAL ASTRONOMER IS YOUR GUIDE.

"I'd like to take a look," Merly said. "How about you?"

Alan said nothing, just sipped his coffee. But the astronomer had overheard Merly. "I'll let both of you look for twenty," he said, shifting his weight from one foot to another.

"That's okay, boss," Alan replied. "I've been to the moon lately and I just got back."

But Merly got up and handed the astronomer fifteen dollars. The man peered through the scope and adjusted some settings. "Now remember, even though what you're seeing appears to be standing still, nothing ever is," he said. He straightened up and guided her over to look. "We live in an emergent universe."

Merly looked back. Patrons laughed and cradled their coffee as waitresses squeezed past, delivering the sweet-smelling beignets. Alan was wearing a dress shirt and Jerry Garcia tie, exactly what he had worn last year in this very place. She tried to picture the moment as distant and something that had happened a long time ago, but Alan's presence, the unmistakable brevity of what was left between them, kept her frozen there, all of her insides coiled tight as she stepped over to peer through the telescope.

Train Shots

Three days after his girlfriend broke up with him, P.T. drove his train over a woman stretched out on the tracks. He'd just rolled around the bend leading into Winter Park when he saw her, a pale speck swathed in a bluish-green dress. As he thundered closer, her white limbs snapped clearly into definition and he threw down the emergency brake. The train's skidding to a halt reminded him of playing ball, the rush of sliding into bases, only without the glory. Metal squealed and sparks shot up. But as usual, he was too late. The collision was out of his control. He shut his eyes and braced for the thump as the train devoured the woman and shuddered down the track for another hundred yards before it finally stopped.

After the impact, he asked one of the crew to take over. Police cars were already zooming up alongside the tracks; the emergency brake had sent out an immediate statewide alert. But as soon as his foot touched the gravel, the whole bloody mess felt different than the other times—the people swarming outside quaint storefronts, pointing, and parents shielding children's eyes. At the park's edge, an unkempt man with a scruffy grey beard swayed and cried out obscenities. The officers met P.T. and he gestured without looking, down to the bend where the middle of the train now idled and huffed, and farther down the track to where he first saw the flapping dress. He knew the woman had been young, and he didn't want to see the years of possibility he'd mangled and smashed.

Instead of drifting down to where the police were pitching the yellow tape, he headed in the opposite direction to survey the train's frontal damage. He expected dented metal, the usual. He braced for blood. Only this afternoon, a gold metallic object shimmered in the sunlight, tangled in the undercarriage between the track and front wheels. A shoe. Her sandal. He crouched to free the strappy thing but failed to grab hold. He rocked back on his heels and slid a few inches down the gravel bank.

A policeman hurried over, saying, "What's that? Don't touch any evidence."

P.T. held his face in his hands, fingers slick with tears.

"Expensive shoe," the officer said. "I haven't gone down to see yet, but they told me she's real young. We just called the college. Too much money and too many drugs with those kids. You okay?"

P.T. rubbed his face. "I'll be fine in a minute," he said.

"A replacement engineer's on his way," the officer said. "Why don't you go take it easy? Sit in the park for awhile."

P.T. stared past the officer at the sparkling fountain in the middle of the park. Children's laughter drifted over. He teetered for a moment, and the officer grabbed his shoulder.

"Your supervisor in Jacksonville said they'd arrange a hotel room for you tonight. Pay for your ticket home tomorrow."

"Thanks," he answered. "I'm fine."

"You sure? Let me call the Park Plaza. It's right over there."

"Fine, go ahead," P.T. said. "But I'll be okay." He wandered past the officer and away from the train's heavy breaths, down toward the park.

•

P.T. slumped onto a bench facing the fountain and let the gurgling sound rush over him. When he first started out as a freight engineer nineteen years ago, he hadn't factored in so many deaths—not only the suicides but the accidents, and not only the human lives but the sheer number of animals that he killed by proxy of the train.

He glanced over his shoulder at the tracks. A local news crew had joined the police activity, and a reporter was now speaking in front of the camera, yellow crime tape draped before the lingering train. He turned around just in time for two college girls to clip past with shopping bags, all thick flowing hair and flimsy tops. Their voices rang like high bells. They stopped at the corner to wait for the crosswalk.

"Excuse me," he called out to them. "Would you two come here for a minute?"

The girls stopped chatting and eyed him.

He waved them over until they slowly approached. The shorter of the two had darker hair and a pigeon-toed walk that he found charming.

"Are you two aware that a girl from your school got killed here just now?" he asked.

The taller girl gushed, "Oh my God," and the other one demanded, "Who?"

"I don't know," he said. "But you need to be careful. This is the second college girl I've hit—my train's hit—in a month. University of Delaware's got tracks running near the campus, just like yours. A girl left a bar one night without her friends, stumbled down near the tracks and... just watch your friends, okay?"

"I'm sorry," the one girl said.

"That's terrible," the other girl replied, shifting her pigeon-toed stance. "But I don't have any suicidal friends."

"It's just that I don't know what to do now," he said, resting his elbows on his knees. "What do you suggest that I do?"

Neither of the girls said anything. He stared at his clasped hands and by the time he looked up, the girls were scampering across the brick-paved street.

•

P.T. returned to the train. The officer from before approached, handed him a slip of paper and pointed out the hotel through the park. "And here's your Amtrak ticket for tomorrow, down to Miami," the officer added. "Is there anyone at home I can call for you?"

P.T. shook his head. "I better go on and grab my things."

"You're staying on Park Ave, so you'll have everything right here," the officer said. "Good food, nice park. Plenty of churches within walking distance."

"Thanks," P.T. said. "But I'm not a church type of guy."

The officer smiled. "We've got lots of places to have a drink, too."

P.T. didn't answer, just swung up onto the stairs and boarded the train. As soon as he climbed inside, he felt dizzy. The crew and replacement engineer said some kind words, patted him on the back, but he hardly heard what they were saying. The air within smelled stifling and gritty. He muttered for someone to fetch his duffel bag and toiletries. Then, with his duffel slung over his shoulder, he jumped off and back into the sunshine and clear sky of February, the palm trees rustling overhead and shiny as copper.

As P.T. walked along Park Avenue, a police car pulled up

alongside him.

"Stephen Dubee," the officer said, extending a card out the window. "Call if you need anything. I don't mind, even if I'm off duty."

The officer drove off. P.T. tucked the card in his wallet, underneath the photo of his ex-girlfriend. In the distance he heard the gates clang down in front of the tracks, pictured the red lights flashing as the train crawled to life, picked up, and rushed past him out of sight.

•

It was quarter after four when he entered the lobby of the Park Plaza, a tunnel of polished wood and plush furniture. The receptionist seemed startled as he meandered over to the desk. Then her face melted into ordered sympathy. "You must be the CSX conductor," she said. "I'll get you up to your room right away."

"Engineer," he corrected, but she had already buried herself in a fluster of keys and paperwork.

"How nice of the company to look out for you after something so terrible," she said. "Will you be getting some time off?"

"I just came off leave," he said. "Third person killed in four months. With lots of deer in between."

She stared and slid the room key over.

The hotel was two stories, his upstairs room dark and cool. A balcony overlooked the avenue below, but not the train station—that was one block behind him. He pulled street clothes out of the duffel. Everything wrinkled and casual, nothing suitable for an uppity neighborhood like this one. Outside the creep of traffic picked up as the end of the workday approached. He checked his phone and dialed Shelley, who still didn't feel like his ex.

"Aren't you supposed to be driving right now?" she asked.

"I killed someone today," he said. "A woman. Really young. All dressed up and stretched out on the track."

"Oh, geez," she said, sighing. "I'm sorry. But please stop saying that you killed someone. She killed herself. That's all there is to it. For you it's an accident."

"How is it an accident? I don't believe in that word anymore. Not lately."

"Suit yourself," she replied. "How much time off are you taking?"

"I don't know," he said. "I don't think I can take sitting home on grieve-leave for another couple weeks. Going through all the same crap with the counselors. All I've ever wanted to do is drive trains. But this is getting to me."

"What's getting to you?"

"All the sadness," he said. "It's incredible."

She scoffed. "I'm surprised you've lasted this long. You're such an idealist, P.T. A little boy who just wants to play choo-choo."

"Go play choo-choo. Okay," he said. His eyes boiled with tears. "Wait till I tell that one to the crew. Hell, can't wait to tell the guy who took over the controls for me today." Bitter sobs bubbled up inside him and he let them spill from his lips like steam.

Shelley told him she had to go and hung up.

•

P.T. took off down the avenue wearing jeans and a button-down. Through the trees he eyed the station, the path of railroad ties and track neat as the yellow brick road. Why did he love an occupation so laden with wreckage and blood—the light-footed deer, statuesque cows, and human beings who came crawling around every bend?

Church bells tolled a few blocks down the avenue. He decided to see if the church was open; maybe he'd just sit there in the cool and quiet. The disheveled man who had bellowed at the train earlier now occupied a table at one of the outdoor cafés. The man reminded P.T. of the bum outside Jacksonville who had died right before the college girl in Delaware. The train was thundering along just before evening, like now. An older man in drab, loose clothing stood on the tracks as if to face off with the train. As the brakes squealed, P.T. did not look away. He wanted to see if the bum would flinch or not. Instead the man raised both arms wide and lifted his chin as if to welcome home a god. In the last instant before the train struck, P.T. could see the tilt of the man's thick glasses on his face, his balding orb shining through matted gray hair, the tape binding the seams of his coat.

P.T. hurried on.

The heavy church door gave easily but as soon as he stepped inside, a cacophony of sounds swelled around him: rustling pamphlets, heaving breaths, the measured cadence of the pastor amplified by a microphone. Was this an evening service? He tiptoed inside a few paces more, straining to hear. Then the smell of carnations hit his nostrils. An usher approached him at a mute clip and whispered, "Step aside, please, sir." The whine of bagpipes from right behind jerked P.T. out of the way; a bagpiper had slipped out of the foyer vestry and now marched in slow motion toward the pulpit and the casket below. P.T. could do nothing but flee.

The sun hung low and orange in the west. He rubbed his bare arms; the air was turning brisk. He shifted his weight from one foot to another, punched the crosswalk button a few times, and jaywalked to the other side. He skated through the sidewalk café and past the bum, who was now chatting in earnest to the empty chair across from him. P.T. considered aimlessly shopping, but most of the stores were closing. In the gourmet kitchen place he asked if any of the others stayed open later. "You can try the vintage shop around the corner," the clerk suggested.

The vintage shop smelled like mothballs and potpourri. He roamed through the cozy thicket of circular racks, stopped to rifle through some dinner jackets. A middle-aged woman, blonde hair to her waist, asked if he was looking for something in particular.

"Not really," he said. "But it's a little chilly outside. I could use a jacket."

She stepped up and shuffled purposefully through the hangers. "How about this one?" she asked, holding up an eggplant-colored velour blazer. "Classic '70s. Isn't it fun?"

"For Halloween, maybe," he said with a laugh. But he allowed her to guide him into the jacket.

In the mirror, he studied the jacket from several angles. He rubbed a sleeve, the material like a warm second skin and rich to the touch, so different from the creased cottons he wore every day. The saleswoman reappeared with a white shirt and slim ankle boots in his size, the outfit complete.

The shop's doorbell jingled as he exited. His faded button-down and scuffed shoes were tucked away in a shopping bag, and his mouth curled up slightly until he rounded the corner. There he landed in the bustle of Friday night on the avenue. He broke away from the noisy tables clustered underneath heat lamps and escaped to his hotel.

•

He stowed his work clothes in his room and was surprised by the weight of the duffel bag in his hands. He'd almost forgotten that lightness belonging only to a life in motion, zooming from station to station, depot to depot. How simple life felt, reduced to a suitcase. But for now he needed some food and, hoping he could find an affordable restaurant within walking distance, he descended to the street. This time he shied away from the glitzy avenue and headed in the opposite direction, down a quieter side street. At the end of the block he met up with the tracks. A narrow service road ran alongside the gravel, up to the main thoroughfare, nighttime traffic whizzing by. He guessed he might walk for a bit and see where the shortcut led him.

So he trudged up the dark road along the bare tracks. Cars lined the opposite shoulder, up to where the tracks crossed the main road—an odd place for people to park, he thought. Where the service road ended and the tracks crossed the main road, he came upon a squat building painted with dancing cactuses and lit by an obnoxious yellow sign.

The place turned out to be an intimate dive with cheerful young waitresses in tank tops and a bar packed with margarita drinkers. In silence he devoured a chimichanga and washed it down with a Pacifico. He was sipping the last of his beer when cheers and whistles broke out. The bartenders whipped out bottles of gold tequila and began pouring rows of shots.

"Train shot?" the bartender shouted at him, pinching a small glass between two nail-bitten fingers.

"What?" he shouted back.

"Every time the train goes by, tequila shots are two dollars. You wanna train shot?"

"I don't like tequila," he said.

"Now you do," she said, slammed down the glass and dumped tequila to the brim. "On me."

The red gates clanged down across the intersection and the noise of the train finally cut through the loud bar. The horn blared and the bartender clanged a cow bell hanging from the ceiling in response. Another wave of drunken cheers rippled through the crowd. P.T. clinked shots with the guy next to him and threw the burning liquid down his throat.

He ordered another beer, and before he was halfway through another train blasted by. Once again the bartender rang the bell, gold hoop earrings swinging against her smooth neck, and he pushed his shot glass toward her. A group of college kids milled at the corner of the bar, and he plunged his sloshing shot glass into the middle of their toast. He caught the eye of one of the girls—she and her friend were the two he'd spoken to earlier. They sidled up, all fancy purses and unblinking lashes, margarita glasses held high.

"Are you okay?" the darker brunette asked. Her pigeon-toed stance was even more pronounced in high heels. "It turned out that the girl who killed herself didn't go to our school."

"Oh," he said. "I didn't hear."

"You made us so worried," her friend replied.

"Sorry," he said.

"It must be so hard for you," the tan one said, and to her friend, "We should buy him a drink."

"That's okay," he said. "I was just heading home. Best thing to do is hit the sack and forget about it." He stepped down from his stool and tossed his wallet onto the bar.

"I'm Casey," the pigeon-toed girl said. "And this is Gibson." He stuck out his hand, but Gibson just peered down into the remainder of her margarita and poked at the ice with the straw. Casey squeezed his arm. "We're buying you a drink," she said adamantly. "Fun will make you forget about it."

He slid back onto the seat, somewhat hesitantly. "Do you know who she was?" he asked.

Casey told him the gossip, that the girl was a twenty-one-year-old drug addict who had spent her entire life in Winter Park and waitressed in one of the cafés. A year before, she had slit her wrists and barely survived.

Another train roared past as he fumbled onto his bar stool. The college brunettes ordered shots. "Should we toast in honor of the girl?" Casey asked. He shook his head no. They then proposed a toast to his days ahead. Gibson complimented him on his purple blazer, and he proceeded to get drunk.

It took P.T. a while to notice the ancient Polaroids that wallpapered the ceiling above the bar and the newer, brighter photos of the staff linking arms with customers in holiday party hats, mugs raised. Some sported polo shirts that looked like the kind restaurant servers wore, the establishment's logo embroidered above the heart. His eyes caught on every young woman in a server's shirt. He wondered if one of them was the woman. Why had she chosen him, waited for him to barrel over her, for a quick, surefire death? Because her own hands were too shaky?

"Do you have someone I can call?" the bartender asked.

Until then, P.T. hadn't noticed that the barstools beside him had been abandoned, the two girls chatting away somewhere on the other side of the bar. A sad and empty space had formed around him. He slapped his credit card on the counter and scanned the bartender's bare wrists for scars.

"Here," he said, thumbing through his wallet. The old

photo of Shelley gawked back. He flicked Officer Dubee's card at the bartender. "Call him."

•

At first P.T. didn't recognize Dubee in his sweater, jeans, and flip-flops. He staggered over to the squad car and collapsed into the passenger seat.

"Do you always dress like a refugee from the Love Shack and get blitzed when you hit someone?" Dubee asked.

"You don't know nothing about being an engineer," P.T. said. "Officer."

"It's Stephen," Dubee said. "So you think you're the only guy with a brutal job?"

"Well, I'm through," P.T. replied.

"I picked your sorry ass up, didn't I?" Dubee said. "I pissed and moaned while I was getting dressed, but here I am. You're what, forty? Forty-five? What else would you do now but drive trains?"

P.T. fell quiet. They cut through a residential neighborhood and towards the park, then past a corner café under a black awning where servers ducked among outdoor tables. "That's where the girl worked," Dubee said. "I knew her."

"You did?" P.T. asked faintly.

"She waited on me a lot," Dubee said. "Nice girl. Sure didn't say anything about her problems."

"And you saw her like that on the tracks today?" P.T. said. "But you seem fine."

"I stood over and gave her a moment. I said, 'Oh, baby, you stuck it to yourself and everybody else.' Then I kept going with my day. What else is there?"

•

Before going to bed, P.T. leaned over his balcony and watched the avenue below. A rowdy party spread out at a sidewalk café. From the midst of scattered tables and chairs, someone chucked a piñata into the street. A Mercedes creeping by caught the paper donkey and dragged it up to the corner stoplight. By then, patrons were running out, shrieking with laughter, to gather the candy and plastic squirt guns from the piñata's opened belly.

Across the street, the café bum tottered and howled. Had he been somebody once, steady and clean-shaven, of the shiny designer shoe crowd, even? P.T. wondered. Would his jabbering or, perhaps, a single sidewalk jab, send him through the park one evening to meet the train? What twists made a person's feet stay glued to those tracks in the face of a thundering machine, to be either tossed or scrambled?

Trains howled all night as P.T. lay awake in bed, but what kept him up had nothing to do with the girl. The sound caused no dread or regret. He didn't think about Shelley's indifference, or the girls at the bar, or Dubee's parting words. He thought about trains. He stared at the ceiling and thought about trains and counted the minutes until morning, when he'd climb on that homebound line and just stare out the window, losing track of time, enjoying the gaps between cities and stations— the moments of just sailing along in the space between places.

Acknowledgments

I would like to express my gratitude to Vermont College of Fine Arts, where these stories began, and to my teachers there, Douglas Glover, Xu Xi, David Jauss, Domenic Stansberry, and Robin Hemley. To Philip F. Deaver and Pat Rushin, for introducing me to the craft of short fiction early on. To the late Jeanne Leiby, for her friendship and guidance. To Lauren Blakeslee O'Regan, my steadfast first reader. To Burrow Press and the Urban Think Foundation, Susan Fallows, Alex Kent, Shelby Nathanson, and especially my editor, Ryan Rivas. And to Frank Messina and my parents, as always, for their generous support.

VANESSA BLAKESLEE was raised in northeastern Pennsylvania and earned her MFA in Writing from Vermont College of Fine Arts. Her writing has appeared in *The Southern Review*, *Green Mountains Review*, *The Paris Review Daily*, *The Globe and Mail*, and *Kenyon Review Online*, among many others. Winner of the inaugural Bosque Fiction Prize, she has also been awarded grants and residencies from Yaddo, the Virginia Center for the Creative Arts, The Banff Centre, Ledig House, and the Ragdale Foundation. In 2013 she received the Individual Artist Fellowship in Literature from the Florida Division of Cultural Affairs. Find Vanessa online at vanessablakeslee.com.